SHARE ME

A MFM MENAGE ROMANCE

DEREK MASTERS

ALWAYS BOOKED PUBLISHING

To all the girls wishing they could be who they really want to be, this one is for you

DEREK'S DARK DESIRES

Subscribe to my Dark Desires newsletter and get a FREE copy of Riot instantly! Riot is a full-length novel that is only available to subscribers!

Once you have your free book, you will have the advantage of knowing when I will be releasing my next title, when I'm having special deals, and you'll be the first to know the next time I have some cool stuff to give away (you can unsubscribe at any time).

newsletter.derekmasters.com

1

KAYLA

As I hung up the phone, I wanted to scream, jump up and down, or hug the next person I saw. Of course, I was standing in line at Starbucks, so I had to keep myself composed.

I'd just come from a job interview at Odin Manufacturing, one of the biggest factories in the Midwest. They make all types of products ranging from consumer goods to materials for the military. Having never worked outside of office complexes, I thought I was going to be in way over my head. Much to my surprise, the interview was great. It was probably one of the best interviews I'd ever had in my life.

When I was being escorted to turn in my visitor's badge, the woman who had interviewed me told me that they had a couple more interviews and that they'd be making a final decision by the end of the week. It came as a surprise that my phone would ring 45 minutes later with a job offer, but I wasn't about to question it. I was ecstatic and must have made a great impression.

Going back into the workforce was going to be strange. It had been just over 10 years since I'd left my last job where I worked as a receptionist. About to leave for my honeymoon, I was teary-eyed as I said goodbye to everyone I had worked with, knowing that when I returned, I was going to be a housewife.

One year earlier, my husband Dillon graduated from medical school and had become an MD. He worked in a local doctor's office for a year to get his name out there, but what he really wanted to do was start his own practice. We both knew that was going to mean long hours, making it more difficult for us to see one another. It also meant that there would be more money, making the decision to leave my job much easier.

I make being a housewife sound like it's been a bad thing, but I honestly have loved every minute of it. My man, hard at work all day while I was at home keeping everything in order. I looked forward to him coming home each night. I'd have dinner on the table, and we'd talk about his day and our future. It was nice for a long time, but it also got very frustrating. When Dillon and I got married, I had pictured things much differently.

My dreams of being a housewife included being a mother. Since it was just me in the house most of the time, there was really just minor tidying up each day. Other than that, I mostly did a lot of reading and watching television.

What I had really wanted all along was to be a mother. I had it all planned out in my head. I wanted to have one boy and two girls, in that order. That way, my daughters would have a protective big brother to make sure nothing bad ever happened to them. We would spend afternoons in the park or on a big swing set in our backyard before reading them bedtime stories at night.

Instead, the backyard is empty other than two large oak trees in the center of the yard. I've intended to start a garden for the last couple of years, but I don't see much of a point. Anything I grew would end up going bad before being eaten. The dinners I used to make for Dillon began getting fewer and further between. I knew he was working long hours, but it was starting to have an effect on us.

Before I knew it, he was no longer interested in my day, and I stopped asking about his. I had come to accept the fact that his life was all about his practice and that starting a family wasn't even on his radar. There had even been times when I wondered if I was even on his radar. It sure as hell didn't feel like it.

I had lost track of the last time he and I spent any real

time together, and that's just referring to something as simple as sitting on the couch and watching a movie together. I certainly wasn't being taken on anymore. It had been close to two years since he took me out on the town. The only time we even went out to dinner was when he was meeting with pharmaceutical reps, and he wanted me there on his arm.

Our sex life was no longer anything to write home about either. During our first few years of marriage, everything was fun and exciting. We were always experimenting in the bedroom and trying new things. We would get frisky outside of the bedroom just as much as we did inside. We would role play and have lots of fun. Those days were apparently over.

Although our sex life wasn't dead, it was very much on life support. I was lucky if I got laid once a month. On the rare occasions that we did have sex, it had become very routine. It was always the same thing. I'd go down on him for a couple of minutes, he might rub me a bit, then he'd roll me over and screw me in missionary position until he was done. I didn't even get off most of the time anymore, at least not with him. I'd wait until he was asleep and then finish the job myself.

Passion. If there is one thing that I miss the most, it's the passion that he and I used to share together. I love him, I really do, and the last thing I want to do it lose him, but something had to give. I was beginning to go crazy sitting in a house by myself day in and day out, so I went looking for something to occupy my time. I found what I was looking for in a job. I just hoped he would understand.

I knew he had a free spot in his schedule during the afternoon, so I took a deep breath and gave him a call.

"Honey, I have some news for you."

2

DILLON

"What do you mean you got a job? I didn't even know you were looking for a job. How long has this been going on?" I asked her, completely caught off guard.

"I've been looking for something to do for a few weeks now. I wanted to tell you, but you're always so busy, and I didn't want to use the little bit of time that we have together fighting and arguing about this. I don't want you to be mad at me."

"I'm not mad at you Kayla, but I am pretty confused. This feels like it came out of left field. As I said, I had no idea you were even looking for a job. What brought this on?"

"Honestly, I feel like I'm going stir crazy looking at these same four walls every single day. It was one thing when you were home more or when I was able to talk to you throughout the day. Now that it's just me sitting here by myself, I can't take it."

"You know, it isn't exactly my fault that I'm not available to call you throughout the day anymore. We both knew that this practice was going to take up a lot of time once it started to grow. You can't act like you're shocked by this."

"Yeah Dillon, I'm well aware. You've been telling me this for a while now. That doesn't change the fact that I'm lonely. I just went looking for jobs to try to find something to get me out of the house and seeing some faces that aren't mine in the mirror. I didn't even think anything would come of it, at least not this quickly. I just went on an interview this afternoon, and it went well, so they hired me."

"I can't believe you were going on job interviews and I had no clue you were even looking for a job. You've kept me out of the loop on this one."

"You're making it sound like I was trying to hide it from you, but it isn't like that at all. As I said, you're never here so when was I supposed to tell you?"

"Exactly the way you're telling me right now."

"Yeah, anyway, I was calling to tell you because I'm excited about it. I was hoping you could be excited for me as well, but I can see that's not happening. I'm gonna let you go."

"I'm sorry. If you're excited, then I'm excited for you. We'll talk about it more tonight. Love you."

"Okay," she replies. "Talk to you later."

I hung up the phone and sat staring at the receiver. Other than being a doctor, there was one thing I was good at, and that was pissing off my wife. Of course, that wasn't my intention, but I'm not sure how she expected me to react to her news.

When we got married, she was all about being a housewife. She loved it, or at least she seemed to. When we were signing the papers to close on the house, she had a hard time hiding her excitement. All she could talk about was all the things she wanted to do in the house.

She was all about how she would decorate, how she would set up the rooms, all the cooking she was going to do, how she was going to learn to garden so she could prepare meals with fresh produce she grew herself.

I have to admit; she is a beast in the kitchen. For years, I would pull into the garage and could smell what she was making in the kitchen. One day it would be spicy sausage and peppers, the next would be homemade pasta sauce and hand-made noodles. She loved being in the kitchen, and I often wonder how I'm not overweight by 100 pounds.

Over time, all of the little things she used to do began to stop. She went from cooking meals every night, to most nights, to pretty much never. I've never once complained, although I do miss coming home to the food on the table. Not so much because I feel like a woman has to cook for her husband, but because she was so damn good at it.

Kayla's food could rival any restaurant in the area. The restaurants that we mostly live on now since cooking is not one of my strong suits. Takeout, takeout, and more takeout is what we eat now. Dinner plans typically consist of her texting me and telling me what she's picking up and me replying with my order.

We don't even go out to dinner anymore. I used to like to get dressed up to take her somewhere nice at least a couple of times a month, but she isn't interested in that anymore. The only time I can get her to come out is when a pharmaceutical rep is taking me out, and I have to basically beg, plead, and grovel to get her to do that.

I'm not entirely sure what has changed in our marriage. I work long hours, but it isn't like she didn't know what she was getting into. I've always been a hard worker. I worked hard through medical school, and I work even harder to build my practice. I figure working hard now will allow me to enjoy life later. I bank my money so I can retire early and spend my time with my wife.

Now I'm wondering if it's been worth it.

I've always had a plan for our future, and I always assumed she'd be on board with it. While it was never formally discussed, I always figured that once I had the practice thoroughly established, she'd come and work for me in the office. Hell, if she wanted to get out of the house, I could have used the help. I've thought about asking her many times, but she has put some much space in between us, I figured she was enjoying her time at home without me.

Maybe that's exactly what this was all about. Perhaps she wanted to get away from the house altogether. Maybe the life I was giving her wasn't the life she wanted.

I feel like I'm missing something.

Something didn't make sense, and I was trying to figure out what it was. Was my marriage on its last legs and I've just been too blind to see it?

3

KAYLA

My stomach was in knots, and I felt like I was going to throw up. I felt like a kid getting ready to go on their first day in a new school, except the school year was already halfway over, and everyone had already made friends.

I couldn't believe I was about to have my first day of work in nearly a decade. I was so nervous that I couldn't even touch the breakfast I'd made for myself, and I had to force myself to suck down my coffee.

The hours at a manufacturing plant are far different from any of the office jobs I've worked at in the past. I was accustomed to a work day that was a standard 9 to 5, but my new schedule was going to be 11 am to 11 pm, four days per week. I only hoped that there would be some cool people to talk to or that was going to make for some long work days.

I didn't know much about what my day was going to entail. The only thing I knew for sure was that there would be someone with me in the office until 3 pm each day, which is when their shift ended.

If I had to choose a couple of words to describe how I felt as I looked at the clock, it was scared shitless. What was I getting myself into? Why in the hell did I apply to work at a factory? Why in the hell did they hire me? Surely there had to be someone much more qualified who applied. Maybe I was making a huge mistake.

For some reason, I'd gotten up before the sun. It was partly nerves and partly because I wanted to do something nice for Dillon since this was new to him as well. Despite what he might be thinking, my choice to get a job outside of the house didn't have anything to do with him, and I intended to talk to him about that as soon as our schedules meshed up.

Taking a deep breath to calm my nerves, I forced myself to start getting ready to start my first shift. Even though my stomach was twisted up in knots, I figured I'd be starving at some point, so I packed myself a turkey and cheese sandwich, a bag of chips, an apple, and a banana for lunch and threw it all in a cooler along with a couple of bottles of water. I sat the cooler next to the front door, so I wouldn't forget and made my way to the bathroom so I could jump in the shower.

I turned the water on as hot as I could stand it and propped my tablet up on the sink so I could listen to my music while I washed. It was a habit that I'd started when relaxing in the tub and it became an obsession.

I hit shuffle, and the sounds of Hey There Delilah by Plain White T's filled the room. Since it was one of my favorite songs, I hoped that it was an indication that the day was going to go great. Little did I know that my day was going to be ruined before I even made it out of the house.

"All ready for your first day?" Dillon asked, walking into the bathroom as I was drying off.

"I'm not really sure," I replied. "I didn't think I'd be as nervous as I am. I feel like I could vomit."

"There's still time to call them and tell them you changed your mind. It's not like you signed a contract or anything. You can still stay home."

"Dillon, please don't start with me. I know you don't want me to do this, but I need to do it for me. You're gone at the practice all the time, and I'm here by myself. At least this way, I can get out of the house during the week and contribute to the household."

"Have you seen the bank account lately?" Dillon asked with a load of snark in his voice. "We don't exactly need the household to be contributed to. You make it sound like I'm out running around at the bars or something. I'm gone all day for us. I'm gone all the time at the practice because I'm putting in the hard work so we can have anything we want in life. I always thought you appreciated that."

"I do, Dillon. I appreciate it very much, but that doesn't mean I don't get lonely."

"Do I need to remind you're the one who said you wanted to be a housewife? You were so excited and used to tell anyone who would listen that you get to take care of the house while your man works to pay the bills. Hell, when we were dating, you told me that you were old fashioned and dreamed of being a housewife."

"That was always my dream, but this wasn't at all what I had in mind. When I said I wanted to be a housewife, I imagined being a wife and a mother. I pictured my days being spent playing outside with our children, preparing their meals and cleaning up after them. I never dreamed that I'd be a housewife in a house all by myself."

"Kayla, we have gone over this time and time again. There's a time for kids, but this isn't it."

"Well, I have a feeling that that time has passed anyway, so it doesn't really matter anyway."

He sat in silence, looking at me as I dried my hair and got dressed for work. It felt weird getting dressed in jeans and a t-shirt since every job I'd ever had required me to be dressed in business attire except for the occasional casual Friday's.

Even weirder was having to put on a pair of steel-toed work boots. Although I technically had an office job, there were going to be times when I had to walk around the plant, so the footwear was required. They were a lot different from the pumps I used to choose for comfort and style. These boots were not only uncomfortable, but they were ugly as hell.

Dillon remained silent, looking down at the tile, not sure what to say. If there was one thing he was used to, it was getting his way. Throughout life, he got what he wanted. It was never handed to him, and he had to fight and claw for everything he had, but in the end, he was used to getting his way. I could see the fact that he wasn't winning this one was eating at him. Part of me felt guilty, but a larger part of me was utterly annoyed.

"So what is this all about?" he asked as I finished curling my hair and was starting to put on my makeup.

"What's all of what about? I'm not sure what you're asking."

"Well, you're going to work in a factory, right?"

"Yes," I replied, hoping the conversation wasn't heading in the direction that I thought it was.

"Aren't most factories dirty and dingy?"

"I guess so, although this place is actually really clean. Besides, I'm wearing jeans and a t-shirt. It's not like I'm dressed in any of my nice clothes."

"That's not what I'm talking about, Kayla. What's the deal with the hair and makeup?"

"You have a problem with me wanting to look nice on my first day of work?"

"Not necessarily, but let me ask you a question. How many women work at this factory?"

"I don't know, Dillon. I haven't started yet."

"Okay, but you were there for your interview, right? How many women did you see?"

"I don't know, a few?"

"Right, a few. That means the majority of the people that are going to be working there are men, right?"

"I guess so."

"Exactly, so don't play me for a fool. The hair, the makeup, you're doing that all so you can look nice for the men at work."

"Are you fucking crazy? You do realize that I'll be working in an office with another woman, right? I'm getting made up to make myself look good, not because I'm going to be around a bunch of guys."

"I'm sure that has nothing to do with it."

"What is the matter with you today? I get that you're upset about all of this, but what have I ever done to make you think that I would be unfaithful or try to get the attention of other men?"

"Nothing, I suppose."

"No, I'm not going to accept that answer. You've obviously got something in your head so why don't you tell me what it is? Why makes you think that me doing my hair and makeup has anything to do with the guys I'll be working around?"

"Honestly? Why don't you tell me when the last time you did your hair for me was? What about the last time you put on your makeup to look good for me? You stopped doing all of that shit for me a long time ago. Even when we go out with drug reps, you pull your hair back into a ponytail, and that's it. You're getting more made up to go into a building full of strangers than you've done for me in years."

I was getting furious but was trying my best to keep my composure. The last thing I needed was to get upset and start crying before my first day. It would wreck my mascara.

"I can't do this right now, Dillon. I can't believe you would want to do this right now."

"You're right, I'm sorry."

"I'm sure you are," I said through gritted teeth as I stormed out of the bathroom, grabbed my things, and made my way towards the front door.

"Try to have a good first day at work," he yelled as I was slamming the front door behind me. I responded with a middle finger in the air that he couldn't see unless he had developed x-ray vision.

I had to sit in my car for a few moments before I could start it. I felt like he'd just started the fight with me in an attempt to ruin my first day. That had to be it, right? But the things he was saying, was he wrong?

4

DILLON

I shouldn't have been surprised. My penchant for fucking things up and making small matters huge was on full display that morning.

There was no ill will or any intention of starting an argument before she left. We hadn't had much time to talk lately, and I wanted to see her off to work since I didn't have any morning appointments.

My first instinct was to feel bad for upsetting her. I thought about sending her a text message since I was sure I wouldn't be able to get her if I called her. I even picked my phone up and entered my passcode to unlock it before becoming disgusted with myself and putting it back down on my desk.

I was tired of always being the one who had to apologize. I was sick and tired of everything being my fault. It wasn't like anything that was coming out of my mouth was a lie. She didn't do her hair for me anymore. She didn't put on makeup for me like she used to. She didn't do anything anymore.

What was worse is that I wasn't supposed to ever bring it up. Anytime I even hinted at the subject; she would change the topic to something completely different. She tried to be subtle about it, but I knew exactly what she was doing.

I listened for her to start her car and leave before I left the house. I didn't have it in me to fight anymore right then. I had a few afternoon appointments and wanted to go ahead and get into the office so I could try to clear my head. I sure as hell wasn't going to be able to do that at home.

I had three patients that afternoon, and I treated them professionally as always, but my mind was definitely on my wife and the argument at home. The more I thought about it, the more I began to wonder if I hadn't been wrong all along.

Maybe I really was an asshole. She'd been staying at home for our entire marriage, cooking and cleaning an almost constantly empty house. I thought women loved a hard worker, but I also understood the concept of being lonely. Maybe getting out of the house and working would be good for her. It would give her some human interaction and allow her to talk to people instead of sitting alone all day.

———

It was bizarre walking into a dark, empty house. Usually, Kayla would have her music playing, and the aroma of whatever she was cooking would hit my nose before I even made it through the door that connected the house to the garage.

The feeling was almost surreal as I placed my keys in the small glass bowl that we kept on a tiny table next to the door and they clinked off the bowl instead of falling on top of hers. The sound echoed throughout the house.

I hadn't eaten since early that morning, and I was starving. I was debating between pizza and Chinese when I opened the door to grab a beer and saw a large dish inside with a note on top of it. I grabbed the piece of paper and opened it up.

Sweetheart,
I know that you don't like the idea of me going back to
work and I just wanted to thank you for not giving me a

hard time about it. I know you're used to dinner being on the table when you get home and although this isn't quite on the table, I hope it gets the job done. Throw this in the oven for 20 minutes at 350 degrees. There's some of that cheese garlic bread that you like in the freezer. I hope you had a great day at work. See you tonight.

Love always,

Kayla

I pulled back the foil and saw that she'd made lasagna, my favorite dish. If I wasn't already feeling like a schmuck before, I sure as shit was after reading that. I never denied the fact that Kayla was an amazing woman. On her first day of work, she got up early, prepped and cooked an entire lasagna just so I'd have dinner when I came home.

Sighing, I grabbed a beer, turned the oven on and sat down on the couch. I really was a lucky man. Sure, she and I hadn't been on the same page for quite a while, but we still loved each other. At least I thought we did. I know that I loved her, but was she still feeling the same about me, especially after the fight that morning? The note said love always, but I couldn't really remember the last time she told me she loved me without me saying it first.

I had another beer once I popped the lasagna into the oven and grabbed one to have with dinner once it was done. Kayla hated it when I drank beer with dinner. I could almost hear her telling me how unsophisticated it was as she grabbed a bottle of wine like she had done during countless dinners over the years.

What the hell, I thought to myself before walking over to the wine rack and grabbed a bottle of Rioja Crianza, a wine that my wife would describe as a medium-bodied red wine, whatever that means. I popped the cork, poured a glass and sat down to have my dinner.

It only took one bite for me to realize what a jackass I'd been that afternoon. Here I was giving her shit over something as petty as her hair and makeup after she'd taken the time to make a lasagna for me for dinner. I made a mental note to apologize for the fight and thank her for dinner. It tasted much better than whatever take out I would have been eating otherwise.

As I ate, I started to wonder about how Kayla's first day of work was going. I hoped that she had been able to put our fight out of her mind and at least try to have a good day. It would suck if her first day ended up being shitty because of my stupid insecurities.

When I finished eating, I put the leftover lasagna back in the fridge so Kayla could have some when she got home, rinsed my plate and stuck it in the dishwasher, and downed the rest of my wine before putting the wine glass in with the plate.

Not knowing what else to do, I grabbed the remote

and sat down on the couch to see if there was a game on. Before I could even turn on the television, my mind went straight to Kayla. More specifically, I started thinking about the fact that she had got a job at a factory where most of the other employees were men. Men who I'm sure would have no problem flirting with a cute girl like my wife.

I knew for a fact that my wife would never cheat on me, but that didn't stop the jealous feelings from developing deep within my gut. I closed my eyes and could just imagine all the men introducing themselves to her. Maybe they shook her hand, or maybe they greeted her with a touch on the shoulder or arm, a touch so insignificant but carrying so much meaning. I could guarantee that they were checking out her ass as she walked away. That is one of her best features after all.

Rubbing my eyes and shaking my head, I tried to get the images out of my mind. The last thing I needed was to let these feelings fester in my head and lead me to overreact to something that wasn't even there. Sitting on the couch wasn't going to help me do that.

I looked down at my watch and saw that it was only 8:00 pm. The shift she'd been hired for was from 11:00 in the morning to 11:00 at night, so it was still going to be quite a while before she got home.

Lately, I've retired to our office after dinner to jump

on the computer. I've always told Kayla that I have patient files to catch up on, but it isn't true. Since our sex life has been on life support, I've gone up to the office to relieve myself. Even though she has a desk and computer in the office as well, she always reads after dinner, so I never had to worry about being caught.

I started to walk towards the stairs that lead down to our finished basement, which is where our office is located, but I realized I didn't have to do that tonight. Instead, I grabbed my laptop and made my way to our bedroom. If the house was empty, I was going to take advantage of it.

I made myself comfortable on the bed, opened my laptop and logged into my favorite porn website. It's not your typical site, though. It caters to a very specific fetish. A fetish that I've kept to myself for the years since I've discovered it. A fetish that I wouldn't dare tell anyone I was into.

I surfed through the videos for about 15 minutes until I found one I liked. It's not bad enough that I'm into a very specific fetish, but I also need the woman in the video to look a very specific way or else I can't get into it.

Once I found what I was looking for, I slid out of my pants and pulled my cock out of my boxer briefs. Watching videos like the one on my screen made me so hard. I paced myself to match the 20-minute video, only climaxing when the man pounding the woman did.

There was something extra relaxing about being able to relieve myself in bed instead of down in my office. I put my laptop on the floor and turned on the television so I could find something to watch until Kayla got home.

5

KAYLA

I felt like I was in a maze as I tried to remember how to get back to the time clocks so I could punch out and go home for the night.

"You did a great job tonight, Kayla," a voice said from somewhere in the darkness.

"Thanks," I replied, having no idea who I was talking to. "Hey, I don't remember how to get to back to the time clock."

"Follow me; I'm out of here for the night too."

Emerging from the darkness was Mark, one of the men who had been showing me around the plant earlier. He was sweaty and dirty from working with the machines, and his t-shirt was clinging to the muscles in his arms. I caught myself staring and forced myself to look away.

Mark smirked, and I could feel my face beginning to

blush. He was younger than me by almost a decade, but he was extremely attractive. He had piercing blue eyes and the kind of soft smile that I'm sure made many women putty in his hands.

"So how did your first night go?" he asked.

"I think it went about as well as it could have. I've never even stepped foot in a factory before, much less worked in one."

"I could see how it would be confusing to someone who's never been in one."

As we got closer to the back offices where the time clock was located, I was amused by how bright the hallway was in contrast to the darker factory. It was like the proverbial light at the end of the tunnel.

"Thanks for bringing me back here," I told Mark as I slid my time card into the slot.

"It's no problem at all. Were we nice enough to get you to come back tomorrow or did we scare you off for good?"

"Oh, I don't know," I giggled, instantly embarrassing myself. "I guess I'll decide that on my car ride home."

"I see. Well, if you decide to come back, I'll show you a trick to know how to get around here. Believe it or not, there is a method to the madness as far as the layout goes."

"Sounds good. I'll see you tomorrow."

"It's a date then," he said, extending his hand for me to shake.

When I reached up, I noticed that he was checking out my ring finger, which was completely bare at the moment. I always remove my jewelry when I take a shower, and after the fight with Dillon that morning, I'd forgotten to put any of it back on.

Noticing him looking at my ring finger made me look down at his. There was no ring on his either. I could have told him I was married right then, but what if his looking at my hand was all in my head? Maybe I was just hoping he was looking because it would be fun to get some form of attention from a man since my husband sure as hell doesn't pay any attention to me anymore.

Mark walked me back to the front of the building, where I grabbed my lunch box and the bundle of papers that had been given to me by human resources.

———

I hoped that the fight Dillon and I had that morning would be blown over by the time I got home. There were a few times at work that I'd debated calling him to tell him that I may have overreacted, but I decided giving him a little bit of space was probably a much better idea.

During the drive home, I reflected back on the first

night of my new job. I had been under the impression that it was strictly office work, but there was a lot more to it than that. I also had to walk around the plant several times, stopping in at all the different departments to see if any outstanding issues needed to be attended to. If so, I opened a ticket to take care of whatever needed to be taken care of.

In many ways, I enjoyed the fact that I wasn't stuck in the office all night. Sure, I got lost in the plant several times and had to ask people where the hell I was, but I got to talk to so many people and have actual conversations.

Dillon had been right about one thing. The factory was a complete sausage fest. I knew that the majority of employees there would be men simply due to the type of physical work that is done there, but I had no idea how skewed the numbers would be. On the 11 am to 11 pm shift, I was one of only three women in the entire plant. It was crazy, and while I planned on telling him all about my first day, that was a piece of information I was going to keep to myself.

As I pulled my car into the garage, I was surprised by how excited I was to tell my husband about my night. I worried that he might not care or may not want to hear it, but I'd never know if I didn't talk to him.

When Dillon and I first met, and for several years after getting married, we were basically best friends. We spent all of our free time together, talked non-stop, and could not get enough of each other. I wondered where things went so wrong. I missed our talks about nothing at all that would last for hours and all the fun we used to have together and wondered if it was gone forever or if there was any way we could ever get it back.

Thinking about the state of our marriage caused tears to begin welling up in my eyes, which was the last thing I wanted. There would be time to talk about our marriage later. On that night, I wanted everything to be happy.

When I walked into the house, the house was dark except for the small foyer light, which Dillon must have left on for me. Figuring he was downstairs in his office, I put my things down on the table and made my way down, but I could see it was dark down there before I even got to the bottom of the stairs.

"Honey?" I called out, wondering where he was, but I was met with only silence.

It wasn't until I made it to the living room that I heard the faint sounds of the television coming from the bedroom. I poked my head in and saw him sleeping soundly. He must have fallen asleep watching sports high-lights or something. He looked so cute and peaceful. I decided that when I climbed into bed, I was going to scoot right up to him and fall asleep on his chest, something that we hadn't done in as long as I could remember.

Starving, I walked back into the kitchen to have some of the lasagna I'd made for Dillon. I was honestly surprised to see that he'd left a note just like I'd made for him.

Sweetheart,

Thank you so much for taking the time out of your day to make sure I had something to eat when I got home. You didn't have to do that, but I'm grateful you did. You and I both know that when it comes to cooking, it was not a skill I was blessed with. You on the other hand...

The lasagna was delicious, and I even had a glass of wine with it because you would have made me do the same had you been home.

I feel like a giant jackass about what happened this morning and think we should make some time to talk. Tonight, I just want to hear about your day. I'll be in the bedroom waiting to hear all about it.

I love you, babe,
Dillon

The note made me feel something that I hadn't felt in a long time: butterflies in the pit of my stomach. In the back of my mind, I knew this sweetness probably wasn't going to last, but I was going to hold on to the feeling as long as I possibly could.

I thought it was also sweet that Dillon had planned on waiting up for me because he actually wanted to know how my first night of work went. No matter what kind of issues we'd gone through, I still loved that man and knew we could get through whatever was put in front of us. Of course, I'd been wondering if he felt the same, but seeing what he wrote to me was a bit of needed reinforcement.

While I ate, I started going through all of the paperwork that had been given to me when I arrived at work that afternoon. There were your typical handbooks, policies and procedures, phone logs, contact numbers, and things like that.

Near the back of the manilla folder, I found all of the paperwork about benefits. There was medical coverage from day one, and while my husband is a doctor, it would come in handy if I was ever in any kind of catastrophic accident that would require extended hospital stays and things like that. It would basically mean not having to go bankrupt while I recovered.

There was also information about investments, 401k, other retirement plans, and things of that nature. Since I hadn't worked in so long, I decided I was going to set aside additional money out of each check to try to catch up.

I needed to go online to pick which plans I wanted to

opt into so I figured I'd go down to the office and jump on my computer to take care of that before I went to bed. First and foremost, I wanted to relax. I thought about slipping into a hot bubble bath, but I really just wanted to be close to my husband, so I opted to creep into our room and put on some comfortable pajamas.

When I turned to walk out of the room, I noticed that Dillon's laptop was lying on the floor next to his side of the bed. Instead of having to walk downstairs, I decided to just use his computer right there in bed.

After putting in his "secret code," code, which just consists of the two of our names together, the laptop came to life. It took a minute for my mind to register what was on the screen in front of me, but once I figured it out, the computer slipped from my hands and fell onto the mattress.

He's been looking at porn. Fucking porn! I'm not a prude by any means, but I haven't been getting any attention in the bedroom, and I felt like I'd just discovered the reason why. He'd rather look at porn than have sex with his wife. That made me feel so shitty about myself and had me questioning what I was doing wrong.

I took a deep breath and composed myself before picking the laptop up off the mattress. I wanted to see what was taking my place. I needed to see what kind of porn was so important that he'd rather jerk off watching it than having sex with me.

The name of the website was "Real Cheating Wives," and it seemed to revolve around videos where the wife is cheating on her husband.

I wondered what kind of sick thrill he was getting out of that. Earlier that day he was giving me shit about the fact that I was doing my hair and makeup for work and then he was watching videos where the wife was cheating. Did he think I got this job to find men to cheat on him with? Was that something that turned him on in some sick way?

What was I supposed to do? I wanted to wake him up and ask him what his problem was. I wanted to know why he was looking at that kind of thing when I was right there whenever he wanted. What was he getting out of the porn that he wasn't getting with me? I really wanted to do that, but I didn't. I needed to sleep on it so I could figure out the best way to handle it.

I did want to know exactly what he was watching so I muted the volume and pressed play on the video had up. There was one thing that immediately jumped out at me. The cheating wife in the video looked exactly like me.

6
DILLON

Panic instantly started to set in as I looked over at the nightstand and saw that the clock read 6:44 am. I had appointment starting at 8:00 that morning and intended to be up at 5:30.

Unfortunately, I'd fallen asleep while waiting for Kayla to come home and didn't get a chance to set my alarm. I stretched and rolled over only to find that she wasn't in bed with me. Sometimes she had trouble sleeping so I didn't think anything of it and figured I'd find her in the kitchen drinking coffee.

I grabbed a fast shower, brushed my teeth, and got dressed in record time, leaving me about twenty minutes about twenty minutes before I had to leave the house. I planned to use that time to see how Kayla's first day at work had been, but when I walked into the kitchen, she wasn't there.

Wondering where she could be, I looked around the house and found her sleeping on the couch wrapped in one of the blankets we usually reserve for guests. At first, I thought that she might have fallen asleep reading or watching television, but the tv was off, and there wasn't a book to be found.

Surely she couldn't be that upset about the fight we had, could she? Sure, we've had our fair share of fights and arguments over the years, but never one that's been so bad that one of us slept on the couch.

"Kayla?" I whispered into her ear, nudging her gently from her sleep. "Kayla, wake up."

"Huh? What? What time is it?"

"It's about 7:20. How come you're sleeping out here?"

"I don't know. I was just lying here thinking, and I guess I fell asleep."

She wasn't fooling me. I knew she was lying. If she ever wants to relax on the couch, she has a throw blanket that she always grabs. She had to go down to the basement closet to get the guest blanket she was using.

"Thanks for the lasagna last night. It was delicious."

"Yeah, I saw the note you left," she replied coldly. The way she said it made me very uneasy. I guess the fight was worse in her mind than it was in mine.

"How was your first night at work?" I asked, trying to sound as genuine as possible.

"Dillon, you don't have to feign an interest. You can save your breath."

"I'm not feigning any interest, Kayla. I'd really like to know."

"It was fine."

"Look, I'm really sorry about everything I said yesterday. I didn't mean for things to blow up like they did. I never imagined it would have you sleeping on the couch."

"Yeah, that's why I'm sleeping on the couch," she scoffed with just a hint of a laugh in her voice.

"If that's not the problem, then what is it?"

"It's nothing. Don't worry about it. Don't you have to get to work?"

"Yes, but not until you tell me what's on your mind. What did I do?"

"What did you do? I don't know, Dillon. Why don't you tell me what you did?"

I searched my brain for anything that could have pissed her off this much. I put my dinner dishes in the dishwasher and put the lasagna back in the fridge. I had no idea what I could have done to make her so angry with me.

"I have no idea. I really can't think of anything."

"Okay, then there's nothing to talk about."

"Fine, I don't have time for this. Whatever it is you're mad about, I guess we can discuss it later."

I turned to grab my things and was almost to the door that separates the house from the garage when she spoke up.

"I used your laptop last night."

My breath caught, and my heart felt like it stopped beating inside my chest. She didn't have to say anything else because I already knew what she meant. I just had to figure out how to downplay it.

"Kayla, you shouldn't get mad about seeing porn on my laptop. All men look at porn."

"Yeah? Even men who are always so tired that they usually have no interest in doing things with their wife?"

"It isn't like that at all."

"Then what is it like? It seems to me that my schedule works out perfect for you. You can lay in our bed and jerk off all you want. No nagging wife to worry about then, huh?"

"You're making this seem way worse than it is."

"Am I, though? I don't think I am. It's not even so much the fact that you were looking at porn that bothers me. I could not possibly care less. If you think I never look at porn, you're nuts. I'm more bothered by the fact that you're watching porn about wives who cheat on their husbands."

"Oh, that's what you're upset about? It just happened to be the video I clicked on. They aren't all like that."

"Dillon, you know me well enough to know that I'm not stupid. I didn't just look at what video you had up. The whole damn website was about cheating wives. I can't believe you would be looking at that, especially after all the shit you gave me yesterday about getting all made up to go to work. Is that what you think I'm doing? Do you think I took this job to cheat on you?"

"No Kayla, it's not like that at all. I just like some of the storylines in the videos on that site."

"Okay, explain one thing to me then. Why did the girl in the video you were watching when you closed your laptop look exactly like me."

Fuck, I was busted. I knew she paid attention to every little detail about everything, but I was really hoping that she wouldn't put that together. If I was ever going to come clean, it was right then.

"All right, listen. I don't think you took your job to cheat on me and I don't believe that you would cheat on me anyway, there's just this fantasy I've always had since we got married, but I've never wanted to bring it up to you."

"Dillon, you're supposed to be my best friend. You've always told me that there isn't anything you can't tell me. We've done plenty of experimenting in the bedroom so I don't know why you'd be worried about me knowing a fantasy. Those are supposed to be fun."

"This one is a little different, and I'm honestly not sure how you'd react to it, especially seeing how you're responding right now to the fact that I was looking at porn."

"Just tell me. I won't judge."

"Okay, I have this fantasy. It's not a cheating fantasy at all because I'd never want you to actually cheat on me, but I've always had a fantasy of watching you with another man."

7

KAYLA

Did I just hear him correctly? Did Dillon just tell me that he's always had a fantasy of watching me be with another man?

"You want to watch me with another man? What does that mean exactly?" I asked, sure that I must have heard incorrectly.

"It's just a fantasy, Kayla. We don't have to make such a big deal out of it."

"We've both had lots of fantasies, though, and we've had no problem acting on them. How long has this been in your head?"

"Always."

"Always? So you've always wanted me to fuck somebody else?"

"Yes. No. Well, not exactly. It's not quite that easy."

"What do you mean it's not that easy? Do you or do you not have a fantasy of wanting to watch me fuck someone else? That's what you said, and that's what the website you were looking at was showing."

"It's a fantasy, Kayla. I think you're incredibly sexy and would love to see you being pleasured from the outside. It's something I never get to see."

"Bullshit. We've made plenty of tapes together. You can watch those if you want to see me pleasured."

"I've watched those tapes so many times. That's what got this fantasy going. I just would like to see it live. That's all."

"I can't believe this. Don't you have to be getting to work?"

"Yeah, but I can push my appointments back a bit so we can talk."

"No, don't. I don't want to talk about this anymore, at least not right now. I'll be at work when you get home so why don't we just talk about this tomorrow?"

"Okay, if that's what you want. This isn't as bad as you're making it out to be."

"Please don't tell me how to feel. Get to work, and we'll talk about tomorrow."

"All right, I'll see you tomorrow. I love you," he said as he walked over to kiss me.

"Love you too," I replied, turning my head, so his kiss hit my cheek instead of my lips.

I stood there while he gathered his things and walked out the door before crumbling down onto the couch. My heart was racing, and I could feel a tension headache forming behind my eyes.

None of what he was saying made any sense. How did he get so jealous the day before and then come home and watch porn about me cheating on him? No matter how hard I tried, I couldn't make myself comprehend it.

I needed someone to talk to about this, but I didn't want to speak to any of our immediate mutual friends. I was sure that he wouldn't want anyone in our inner circle to know about this fantasy.

Grabbing my cell phone off the coffee table, I scrolled through my contacts list when I came across the perfect name for the situation.

Meghann was my old college roommate, and she was a bit of a wild child back in the day. I had no idea how much had changed, but last I heard, she'd gotten married and had a couple of kids. We kept in touch on Facebook but hadn't talked on the phone for quite some time. I dialed the number and hoped she'd be available to talk.

"Hello?" she answered, sounding as though I was waking her.

"Hey Meghann, this is Kayla."

"Kayla? Kayla Baker?"

"Yeah, it's me. How are ya?"

"I'm doing really well. How are you?"

"I've been better. Do you have a few minutes to talk?"

"Of course. What's going on?"

"Well, I got a new job and started yesterday. When I got home last night, I jumped on my husband's computer to fill out some forms and saw that he'd be looking at porn."

"Porn? No, not that," she sarcastically said with a giggle. "You know everyone looks at porn, right?"

"Yes, I know that. It's not the fact that he was looking at porn that has me concerned. It's the type of porn he was looking at."

"Oh, you found out he's into some weird shit, huh? Was it midgets? I bet it was midgets. Fuck!"

"No, it wasn't midgets. It was cheating wife porn."

"Cheating wife porn? That's it? That's disappointing."

"What? Disappointing?"

"I'm kidding, but I still don't see what the big deal is."

"The big deal is that before I left work, my husband gave me a bunch of shit about the fact that I was doing my hair and makeup to go work around a bunch of men."

"Was he right?"

"Was he right? No. Well, not really. I got a job in a

factory, and most of the people who work there are men, but that's not why I was doing it."

"Is there a reason he would think that's why you were doing it?"

"He says it's because I never do my hair and makeup for him anymore."

"Was he exaggerating or is there any truth to that?"

"Honestly? He was right, but I was just doing it to look presentable on my first night. I didn't have an ulterior motive."

"You know that, but to him, seeing you get made up for other people and not for him probably hurt his ego. You know how men are."

"Oh, believe me, I know. The thing was, it's not just the porn. It's what he told me after I confronted him about it."

"What did he tell you?"

"He told me that his biggest fantasy is to watch me sleep with another man."

"Wow, sounds like you're a lucky girl?"

"Lucky? He got jealous about me doing hair and makeup to go to work but then tells me he wants to watch someone else have sex with me. Have you ever heard of such a thing?"

"Of course, I'm very familiar with it actually. There's even a name for it."

"Yeah, it's called crazy."

"No," Meghann laughed. "There is actually a couple of different names for what you're describing. It could either be called hotwife or cuckold, depending on what the rules are."

"What's the difference?"

"Well, a hotwife situation is when the wife and husband agree to what the rules and limits are. The husband usually has a big say as far as who and when. He also has full veto power. The men in these relationships are referred to as stags, and even though they're sharing their wife, which is known as a vixen, they're still ultimately the alpha in her life and should always be treated with respect."

"Okay, what about the other one?"

"As far as that goes, he would be the cuckold, and you would be the cuckoldress. Cuckolds usually have no say in what the wife does and is often degraded during the sex acts. Some women even put them in a chastity cage and don't allow them any sort of sexual satisfaction."

"Yeah, I don't think that's what Dillon has in mind."

"The whole cuckold thing isn't nearly as common as hotwife."

"I've never heard of either of these things. How do you know so much about it?"

"Oh honey, my husband and I have been living the

hotwife lifestyle for years now. It's a lot of fun getting to experience new partners, but the best part is the reclaiming."

"Reclaiming? What does that mean?"

"Reclaiming is amazing. After I've been with someone else, my husband basically attacks me and ravages me. It brings out some kind of animalistic tendencies in him, and he has to show me that I belong to him. It's literally the best sex I've ever had in my life."

"How long did your husband keep his fantasies a secret from you?"

"He didn't as far as I know. He just came up to me one day and said we should try it. It's actually kind of strange that your husband didn't just tell you what he wanted. Most men who have this fantasy are eager to tell their spouse about it."

"That's what I was afraid of."

"Is something wrong?"

"I have a sickening feeling that there's more to this than what he's telling me."

8

DILLON

My day at the practice seemed to drag on and on. I had trouble concentrating on the needs of my patients because my mind was stuck on the conversation with Kayla that morning.

All day long, I made sure to tell my medical assistants how much I appreciated them because they played a big part in keeping things together. I never lost my professionalism, though. When speaking to a patient, I made sure that my attention was completely on them. If there ever came a time that I couldn't focus, at least when a patient was in front of me, I'd reschedule their appointment before giving them less than stellar care.

Still, I counted down the hours until my last appointment had come and gone. My last patient was still at the front desk scheduling his next appointment as I was slipping out the back door and heading for home.

Once again, the house was eerily quiet when I returned home; the silence is more pronounced than it had on the previous day. Inside the fridge, there was no dinner waiting for me like there had been the day before. There were also no notes left behind for me to read. The differences that 24 hours made were like night and day.

I made a sandwich and picked at it for a while before deciding that I just wasn't very hungry. My stomach was tied in knots, and although I knew I needed to eat something, I couldn't make myself choke anything down. Anything, that is, except for a cold bottle of beer. I grabbed one of those out of the fridge and savored the taste. It went down smooth. Before the night was over, I'd go through plenty more than just that one bottle.

Kayla told me that morning that we could talk about everything the next day, but there was no way I could let it drag on that long. I may have been mentally exhausted, but I was going to be waiting up for her when she got home from work if I had to tape my eyes open.

I tried to find something to keep myself busy. I flipped through the television, thumbed through a magazine, took a hot shower, and drank more beer, but I wasn't able to focus on anything else. My mind kept focusing on one thing: the fact that Kayla was in a workplace that was almost entirely men.

She was mad at me, but mad probably wasn't a word that would do what she was feeling justice. She was furious and probably confused as well. I wondered if she talked to any of the guys she worked with about the problems we were having. I wonder if she mentioned to any of the men about how her husband dropped the bombshell that he wanted her to sleep with other men.

When I closed my eyes, I could picture just that happening. An attractive man giving a listening ear while she spilled her emotions out. I could hear him telling her how crazy it was and how if she were his, he would never dream of letting her be with anyone else. He could tell her that she was beautiful and start the process of moving in on my territory.

Of course, it could have gone the other way as well. She could have shared what I told her, and some other man could use that to his advantage. Perhaps he would tell her that even though it sounded crazy, maybe they should do exactly what her husband wanted her to do.

I could almost see the lust in her eyes as I imagined him whispering into her ear that she should meet him out in the parking lot on their lunch break. I pictured him leading her out to his vehicle, most likely some kind of pickup truck, and being all over her in the cab.

There would be lots of kissing, touching, groping, and exploring. In a moment of confusion and weakness, she'd allow him to slip his hand into her panties while she used her own to feel the bulge forming in his jeans.

Before long, he would have her shirt over her head, unclasping her bra and taking her perfect, hard nipples into his mouth, sucking and nibbling on them just the way she likes. He would then direct her head down to his crotch, releasing his cock and encouraging Kayla to take it into her mouth.

Finally, nice and hard, he would help her shimmy out of her jeans before positioning her on his lap. With her arms wrapped around his neck, she would slide herself down his thick shaft, feeling his hardness while her wet slit gripped onto him. She would grind her hips as she took him all the way in, starting slowly and getting faster, both of them moving rhythmically.

She would be looking directly into his eyes, her moans filling the inside of his vehicle as she moved faster and faster, bringing herself closer to orgasm as she moved. At the same time, she could feel him beginning to swell inside of her.

Bucking her hips faster and faster, she gets herself off, which leads to her already tight pussy clamping down on him, squeezing the cum right out of him. With a shudder, she would kiss him before raising herself off of him, slipping her panties and jeans back on.

For the remainder of the day, she would walk around the factory with him leaking out of her, a constant reminder of what she had done. Would this disgust her or make her want more?

Even though this would be considered cheating and wasn't at all what I wanted when I said I wanted her to sleep with someone else, I was completely aroused. My cock was rock hard as my hand found my way into my pants, gripping it and stroking it up and down.

I wanted to throw my pants off and jerk off while thinking of all the possibilities of what my wife could be doing, but I stopped myself. I needed to have a clear mind when Kayla came home, and if I took care of myself right then, the conversation later might not seem as important. Even worse, it would probably relax me and cause me to fall asleep, which was the last thing I wanted. I needed to get us on the same page, and the longer it took for us to talk, the harder it would be to get us there.

Instead, I got up and grabbed yet another beer from the fridge, allowing it to do its part to take the edge off and prepare me for what was to come.

9

KAYLA

I thought I would hate working 12-hour shifts, but it amazes me how quickly it goes by because I'm so busy. An added benefit to the schedule was the fact that I would get three days off each week instead of the two that most people get.

Getting around the plant was still difficult, and I managed to get lost on more than one occasion, but I was starting to get the hang of it. As promised the night before, Mark was there to help me whenever I got lost.

"Hey, some of us are going out to get a drink. You want to come with us?" Mark asked as we were clocking out to go home.

I have to admit that the offer was very tempting. It would have been nice to have a drink and unwind after a long night at work while enjoying some adult conversation and getting to know some of the people I'd be working with. At the same time, after what had been transpiring at home, I didn't feel like it would be a good idea.

"I wish I could, but I need to get home. I've got a million things to do. Maybe another time?"

"Okay, I'll give you a raincheck, but I'm going to hold you to it."

"All right, you've got yourself a deal."

I clocked out and quickly made my way to my car. That drink really could have done me some good, but with the way I was feeling, I wasn't sure I'd be able to stop at one, and I didn't have a designated driver. Besides, I could just hear Dillon going on and on about me going out with guys after work, regardless of the fact that they were just my friends.

One good thing about my schedule was the fact that there was virtually no traffic on my way home. I remember the days of sitting in rush hour traffic all too well and wasn't missing them one bit.

As I pulled into the garage, I noticed that there was a light coming through the living room window. I wondered if Dillon had fallen asleep on the couch again. He knew that I hated when he did that and I could see him doing it just to piss me off.

He wasn't sleeping, though. He was standing in the kitchen when I walked through the door.

"Hey," he said as I threw my lunch bag up on the table.

"Hey," I replied, feeling weird about what he had told me all over again. "How come you're still up?"

"I wanted to stay up so we could talk. I know I won't be able to rest until we clear the air, so I figure tonight is as good as any time. Of course, if you're tired, I won't make you talk this evening."

In all honesty, I was tired. I was downright exhausted. As I was quickly finding out, there was a ton of walking involved in my position at work. I made a mental note to get myself a pedometer so I could see how many steps I took on any particular night.

Honestly, I was surprised to see Dillon waiting up for me. Seeing him made me wonder if he was still awake for my sake or his. Lord knows it's been a long time since he's put my needs before his own.

A large part of me was thankful that he wasn't in bed. Even though I told him that I needed some time to process what had happened and that we'd talk the next day, I'd already had the past 12 hours to think about it, and I didn't want to wait anymore. I needed some answers.

"No, it's fine. I think this is something that probably shouldn't wait any longer."

"All right, why don't we sit down at the table? Do you want some coffee or anything?" he asked.

"Wine. I'll take a glass of wine."

He went into the kitchen and poured me a glass of Chardonnay.

"So do you want to start?" he asked, placing the wine on the table in front of me.

"Yeah, I think that will be best. I've been thinking about this all night, and I want to know what your end game is."

"My end game? What do you mean?"

"I mean as far as your fantasy goes, what do you get out of it in the end. What is your end game? What's your ulterior motive?"

"It's just a fantasy, Kayla. I don't have any motives. It's just something I've always wanted to see."

"If it's something you've always wanted to see, how come this is the first time I'm hearing about it?"

"Jesus Kayla, what the fuck was I supposed to say? Hey, I love you so much, but why don't we find you a guy to fuck this weekend? We both know how that would have gone. Pretty much the way this conversation is going right now."

"I call bullshit on that. You've never had a problem telling me about any of your other fantasies."

"Yeah, but those were fantasies that only involved us."

"There has to be something more to this. I've been

thinking about it all night while I was at work. Why do I get the feeling that you're trying to trap me?"

"Trap you? How would I be trying to trap you?"

"I was thinking back to before we got married. Your mom insisted that I sign that prenup because you were going to be this big time doctor and I was going to be nothing but a housewife. I specifically remember there being something in the prenup that says if I cheated on you, I'd get nothing if we got divorced. Is that what this is about? Are you trying to trick me into cheating on you because you want to leave me and you're afraid I'll take your money?

"No, it's not like that at all."

"Okay, so are you trying to get me to cheat on you so you can hold it against me for the rest of my life? Do you want me to do something so you can somehow make it out to be like I owe you?"

"No, I would never do anything like that Kayla?"

"If that's not it, then are you having an affair? I know we don't spend much time together. Are you really at the practice all the time like you say or do you have someone on the side? Do you want me to sleep with other men, so you get a free pass to have an affair? Do you want it so I have no right to say anything about what you do or else I'd be a hypocrite?"

"I'm not having an affair. I don't want to be with anyone else but you."

"But it would all make so much sense. Our sex life has been so cold for a while now. If I went out and fucked other men, then you'd have free reign to see whoever you wanted. That's the only thing that makes sense. If you're not wanting to set me up for a divorce, then it has to be an affair. It has to be."

10

DILLON

Kayla was starting to go off the deep end. She was getting hysterical, and there was no reason for it. She was throwing around a lot of accusations, none of which were true. In fact, she couldn't have been further from the truth if she tried.

"Listen to me for just a minute. Really, really listen to me. It seems like you've let your mind go crazy and you've come up with all these scenarios that aren't real. Everything you're saying is just the result of an overactive imagination and thinking in a worst case scenario situation," I told her, hoping it would finally start to sink in.

"Then what is it, Dillon? Help me understand this."

"Look, I'm not trying to trick you in any way. I don't want to divorce you and I sure as hell don't get a damn about that prenup. If you remember, I was very much against it."

"Yeah, but you still went through with it."

"Come on, Kayla. We both know that my mom wasn't going to get off my ass until I did it. I know that you were upset and just signed it when our lawyer put it in front of you, but if you had ever read it in-depth, you'd see that it's the flimsiest prenup in the history or prenuptial agreements. I had it written that way on purpose because even though I'm the doctor, we've both played a huge part in getting to where we are today."

"You've always told me that, but I always thought it was your way to make me feel better."

"No, I've always been straight with you on that. As far as being with other people, I have no desire to be with anyone else."

"That's where I get confused. I don't see why you would want to see me with another man but wouldn't want to be with another woman in return."

"I know that can be confusing, but other women don't appeal to me. You're my girl. You always have been, and you always will be."

"For a long time, I believed that to be true, but somewhere along the way, something happened. You used to look at me like I was the only girl in the world. That changed quite a while ago."

"Kayla, believe it or not, I love you very much. I know I've done a shitty job showing it lately, but that doesn't make it any less real. In all honesty, I think you're the sexiest woman in the world, and there is no way that anyone could compete with you as far as that goes."

"If that's the case, why do you want to share me?"

"The fact that I think you're the most gorgeous woman on earth is precisely why I want to share you. I know you think that this might be some kind of trick so that I can sleep with other women, but that doesn't interest me at all. I don't have any desire to be with any woman other than you."

"Okay, but..."

"Hold on, just let me finish. The reason I want to do this is because I want to watch you be pleasured. I look at that porn that you found to feed into the fantasy. The fact that the woman in the video looked like you was not an accident. I watch it and imagine it's you. I want you to do it in real life so I can experience you being my personal porn star."

11

KAYLA

Everything he was saying was beginning to make perfect sense to me. The videos he was watching were all about wives sleeping with other men. I didn't see anything about husbands sleeping with other women. On top of that, the woman in the video looked exactly like me, a fact that I'd pointed out to him when I found out what he had been watching.

Still, even knowing that this wasn't a trick to set me up for a divorce or for him to be allowed to sleep with other women, I still had plenty of questions. I wanted to be happy that he was willing to share his fantasy with me, but the only reason I knew about it in the first place was because I'd caught him.

"If I asked you a question, would you give me an honest answer?" I inquired.

"Of course. I'll always be straight with you. You should know that by now."

"All right, there's something I'm confused about here. You say that I'm your ultimate fantasy and that you're so turned on by me, right?"

"Absolutely."

"Okay, if that's true and I turn you on so much, why have you been so distant for so long? Why did you stop paying attention to me? Why did you become all about work and start to ignore me?"

"Kayla, are you sure you really want to talk about this right now?"

"Yes, I think about this stuff all the time. I've wanted to ask you for a long time, but I was scared that maybe I didn't want to know the answer. Well, I think I deserve to know what it is about me that started making you act like I didn't exist."

"I'm not really sure the right way to say this because I don't want either of us to leave this conversation feeling bad about ourselves or one another."

"Just say it. Tell me what you feel. This conversation has been a long time coming. We both know it. If we don't get things out in the open now, when are we going to do it? It's not like things are going to get better on their own. We need to talk about this."

"Okay, then I'm just gonna spit it out. The distance

between us isn't all my fault. It takes two to tango and all that."

"Two to tango? What is that supposed to mean?"

"It means I'm not the only person in this relationship that has allowed our marriage to go to shit. You started to shut down long before I did."

"What? I never shut down. I've been the same person since the day we got married."

"Really? You've seen me getting distant but not yourself? Think about how things were when we first got married. We used to go out all the time. You'd get all made up, and I'd take you out to nice dinners and dancing. You used to throw on one of my jerseys and go to hockey games with me. You used to do your hair and makeup when you weren't even leaving the house and when I asked why you were getting all made up, do you remember what you used to say?"

"That I just wanted to look good for you," I replied, trying very hard not to allow my eyes to fill up with tears.

"Yeah, you would put on your makeup and do your hair just because you wanted to look good for me. I never expected it, and I told you all the time that you looked beautiful without it, but you still wanted to do it for me. When you stopped doing it, I took notice."

"I never thought about that."

"I've been thinking about it for a long time. That's

why I made such a big deal about you doing it when you were getting ready for work. I didn't understand why I didn't deserve it anymore, but a bunch of strangers did. It really bothered me."

"I can understand that."

"As far as going out, you put the brakes on that too. You started telling me you just wanted to cook when I asked if you wanted to go out to dinner. If I wanted to take you to a movie, you'd tell me there was nothing out that you wanted to see, which I found strange because you always found new releases to watch on Netflix. The only time I get to take you out is when a pharmaceutical rep is in town, and even then, I feel like I'm pulling teeth."

"Wow, I didn't realize you felt this way. What changed in the bedroom?"

"Are you serious? All of this is what changed in the bedroom. I know you're saying that you've felt unloved and unwanted for a long time, but how do you think I've felt? When you stopped wanting much to do with me in everyday life, I felt rejected. When it came to sex, you used to be up for it all the time, but you started telling me that you were too tired or that you weren't in the mood. I stopped trying because I didn't want to be rejected anymore."

I lost the battle in my fight to hold back my tears as I started sobbing uncontrollably. I was so focused on what had changed with Dillon, that I never even bothered to look at the part I played in our relationship changing.

Even after everything, he hated to see me cry. At the first sight of a tear rolling down my check, he pulled me close to him, kissed me on my forehead and told me everything was going to be just fine. We could work on things if I wanted to. At that moment, I know that working on things was exactly what I wanted to do.

———

It had been a month since we had our talk and decided that all we both wanted was to save our marriage. He started closing the practice one day a week to match my weeknight off.

One thing we committed to was a weekly date night. The rules are simple enough. We would each take turns picking where we went and what we did. While on our date, our phones would be put away and neither of us would talk about work. For one night every week, things were all about us.

For the first couple of weeks, we didn't talk about anything in particular. It was just catching up and talking about everything and not nothing all at the same time, just like we used to do.

During our third date, I decided to ask him about his

fantasy. In many ways, I credit his fantasy for fixing our marriage. If I had never used his laptop and saw what h had been watching, we may not have ever opened a dialog about what we were feeling.

He was very open about his fantasy and didn't have a problem with any questions I asked, regardless of how dumb they were. The more he told me about the fantasy; the more intrigued I became.

Although it was something I didn't ever plan on doing, the thoughts he was planting in my mind were beginning to turn me on. Before I knew it, his fantasy began to consume my thoughts. When he wasn't home, I started going to the websites and watching the videos. I started taking extra long showers so I could masturbate. Slowly, I began to realize that his fantasy was becoming my fantasy too.

12

DILLON

Things between Kayla and I were better than they'd been in years. We were communicating with each other, which was something we hadn't done in quite some time. We were talking, laughing, and enjoying each other's company.

In many ways, I felt like we were given a second chance to enjoy our honeymoon stage, except it was even better this time. After so many years of marriage, most people don't fight for what they have, which is probably why divorce rates are so high. I was thankful that we were able to breathe new life into a relationship that was dying.

An unexpected circumstance of our new lines of communication was Kayla coming around to the ideas of my fantasy. She wasn't eager to go out and actually do it, but she was at least willing to talk about it. I had a feeling that she thought about it more than she was willing to admit, even though she denied it when I asked her about it.

Everything came to a head one night after I had taken her out to dinner and a comedy club, where we both had quite a bit more than the posted two drink minimum. We were lying in bed when she leaned over and started kissing my neck and whispering into my ear.

"I know you like when I kiss on you. Do you think about me lying in bed with someone else, kissing their neck like I do yours?" she asked playfully.

"Yes, I've thought about that a lot."

She moved from my neck to my lips, giving me a deep kiss.

"What about me kissing them, pushing my tongue into his mouth? Maybe even biting their bottom lip the way I do?"

"Mm-hm, I like the sound of that."

Kayla looked down and saw the bulge that had formed in my boxers. I was amazed at how I went from completely soft to rock hard with just a few words out of her mouth.

"You certainly do like that, don't you?" she giggled as she reached down and started rubbing my hard-on through my boxers. "I'm sure if I was in bed with another man, his dick would be just as hard. What do you think about me reaching down and grabbing another man's cock through his underwear and feeling it grow in my hand?"

I had to bite my tongue to the point where it started to hurt just to take my attention away from her touching me because if I didn't, I was going to blow my load.

"Or what if I reached in and grabbed it?" she continued, moving her hand inside of my boxers, gripping my shaft at the base and slowly stroking upward.

"Get over here," I told her as I grabbed her and flipped her onto her back, kissing her deeply and passionately, as though we were horny teenagers making out in the backseat of a car.

This was the first time that she had brought up the scenario in bed, and it was making me hotter than I ever could have imagined it would.

"I want you so bad," she whispered into my ear.

I moved from her mouth and started kissing her down her body, stopping briefly at her collarbone and breasts before making my way between her legs. She grabbed the back of my head to push my face towards her pussy, which was already glistening, but I wanted to try something. It usually took some work to get her off, and I wanted to see if I was right and she was just as turned on by the fantasy as I was.

"For the rest of the night, I'm not your husband. Your husband isn't here. I want you to close your eyes and imagine that you've spent the evening at a bar. Not a cheap, hole in the wall kind of place, but a bar in a nice hotel. The kind of hotel that businessmen frequent."

"Uh-huh," she whispered as I bent down and gave her clit one single lick.

"Now imagine that an attractive businessman has taken an interest in you and has been buying you drinks all evening. As it starts to get late, he invites you up to his room. He tells you he likes talking to you, but you both know that's not what the invite is about."

"Mmmm," she moans as I give her another quick lick.

"He pours you another drink as soon as you get up to the room before he takes a seat and turns on some music. He tells you how sexy you look and asks you to dance for him. You place your drink on a nightstand and start giving him the most erotic dance you can think of. Your dance turns into a striptease. You seductively and provocatively take off every piece of clothing you're wearing except for your g-string panties."

"Keep going," she groans while I slide a finger inside of her tight, wet slit.

"You walk over to the chair he's sitting in, turn your back to him, and lower yourself onto his lap. As you grind against him, you can feel him starting to get hard in his slacks. You turn around, straddling him in his chair, undoing his tie, pulling it off, and throwing it across the room. Not being able to keep his hands off you, he grabs and a handful of your tits and brings your nipples into his mouth."

"Oh God," she says as I slip a second finger into her.

"When he can't take your teasing anymore, he grabs you around your waist, lifts you up and puts you down at the edge of the bed. Forcefully, he spreads your legs, pulls your panties to the side, and shoves his head between your legs, just like this."

Her legs were already beginning to shake before I leaned down and started licking all over her clit. Within 30 seconds, her pussy was starting to grip my fingers tightly, her breathing became shallow, and she grabbed the hair on the back of my head tightly.

"Oh God, Dillon, I'm cumming!"

Her entire body started convulsing as she had the hardest orgasm I can remember her having in quite some time. It was so hard that she became so sensitive, she had to push my head away from her.

"You liked that, didn't you?" I asked.

"Yeah," she replied, giggling as she tried to catch her breath. "That was fucking hot."

I was right. She was fantasizing about it as well. Even if it never happened, it was nice to at least role play and talk about it. If I was never going to be able to actually share her, that was the next best thing.

13

KAYLA

Dillon had an appointment at 8 am so I knew he would be leaving the house early. It wasn't so much that I wanted him to be out of the house, but I really wanted to call Meghann to tell her about what has happened in the past month since I last spoke with her. As soon as his car was out of sight, I picked up the phone and dialed her number.

"Girl, somebody better be dying or bringing me a lot of money for this phone to be ringing at 7:30 in the morning," Meghann mumbled into the phone.

"Good morning to you too sunshine!"

"Oh God, you're one of those happy and chipper in the morning people."

"Yeah, yeah, do you have a minute or do you want me to call you back later?"

"It depends on what you want."

"I wanted to talk to you about what we talked about last time I called you."

"Oh, about your husband wanting you to fuck other guys?"

"That seemed to have perked you up."

"What can I say? I love the juicy stuff. So what's going on?"

"Would it be weird if I said that I think finding his porn may have saved our marriage?"

"Maybe a little. I'm going to need more details than that to make a decision."

"Well, finding the porn initially led to a big blowout fight that I was sure would be the end of us. Instead, it resulted in a long conversation about what was missing in our marriage and what we needed to do to fix things."

"That's a good start. What did you come up with?"

"We've both drifted apart from each other, and we both thought it was the other's fault. We didn't look at what we were doing ourselves to push the other away. We decided to have one date night each week that's only about us."

"That's sweet, and I'm happy for you, but you did not wake me up for all this kissy sweet shit did you?"

"Jesus, I'm getting to the good stuff," I laughed. "Reconnecting has allowed us to talk openly about his fantasies and things like that. I've got a much better idea of what he fantasizes about."

"That's a good first step. What did you find out?"

"First of all, he has no interest in sleeping with anyone else himself, and he made that clear right up front. He says that I'm the most beautiful woman in his mind and he wants to watch me be pleasured. He told me that he wants me to be his own personal porn star."

"Did he mention wanting you to make fun of him or degrade him or anything like that? Anything about not sleeping with him anymore and only sleeping with other men?"

"No, nothing like that. He still wants me very much."

"Good, that means you don't have a cuckold situation on your hands."

"I'm assuming that would be bad?"

"It's not my cup of tea, but some people like it. It's more for dominant women and men that have a secret sissy side. Most women in a cuckold relationship put their man in chastity and don't give them any pleasure."

"Dillon is definitely not a sissy. I don't see why people would be into that. What could the man possibly get out of it?"

"The hell if I know. I like being in control now and then, but I get off on my man getting off."

"Yeah, I know what you mean. So this is the other

thing you said on the phone last time. What was it called?"

"Honey, you've got yourself a full-fledged hotwife situation on your hands. You're a lucky girl. I can't tell you how many of my friends are jealous because I'm in a hotwife relationship."

"Wait a minute. Are you telling me that your friends actually know about it?"

"Not all of them. Just the ones I can trust not to tell everyone my business."

"I don't think I'm going to tell anyone but you."

"Oh, so you're going to go through with it?"

"What? No, that's not what I said."

"You just told me you weren't going to tell anyone. That would insinuate that there was something to tell."

"I don't know what to do, Meghann. We've been talking a lot about it, and it really turns him on."

"What about you? Does it do anything for you?"

"Honestly, the more we talk about it, the more it becomes my fantasy too. I'm just scared that if I do it, he'll regret it or something and it will break us for good."

"I have a feeling that's something you won't have to worry about. If you'd like, I'd be more than happy to show you the ropes."

"What do you mean? I'm not ready to do this just yet."

"You don't have to do anything you're not ready for. Why don't the two of us go out clubbing this weekend? I'll take you to a couple of my favorite spots and show you how easy this is if you want to pursue it. It'll just be a girls night with no pressure to do anything you don't want to do. We'll have some drinks, dance, and let all the boys eat their hearts out."

"Do you know how long it's been since I've been clubbing? Probably before I got married. That sounds like fun. Let me run it by Dillon, but I can't see him having a problem with it. I'll call you back this evening."

———

Dillon was almost asleep when I came home from work, but I'd been thinking about my phone call with Meghann all day, so he was just going to have to wake up and talk to me.

"Babe, are you asleep?" I asked, knowing that he was right on the edge.

"Almost, what's up?"

"Do you remember my friend Meghann from college?"

"Vaguely, why?"

"Well, I called her today and was telling her about what we've been talking about lately."

"What? You mean about the fantasy? Why would you tell anyone that?"

"She's the only person I've told. Besides, if you remember her at all, she was always the slut of the group. Apparently, not much has changed except now she's a married slut."

"I don't understand what you're telling me."

"Okay, do you know that what you want me to do is called being a hotwife?"

"Yeah, I've heard the term."

"Good, because Meghann is a hotwife. Her husband has the same fantasies as you, and she acts on them. He loves it apparently. Well, she wants to get together this weekend, and I just wanted to make sure you were okay with it."

"Sure, I'm fine with it. Why wouldn't I be? What are you girls going to be doing?"

"She wants to go clubbing."

"Clubbing? You want to go clubbing?"

"What's wrong with that?"

"Nothing, I just can't picture it."

"I'll have you know that I used to go clubbing quite a bit. She said she's got a couple of spots that she likes to go to. She offered to show me the ropes."

"Show you the roped of what?"

"Show me the ropes of being a hotwife."

14

DILLON

There was something extremely sexy about watching Kayla getting ready to go out clubbing with her friend. This was especially true knowing that the friend she was going out with was a promiscuous hotwife herself.

"So what kind of trouble are you crazy women going to get into tonight?" I asked Kayla playfully.

"Probably not the kind of trouble you're hoping I'll get into so settle down," she joked back. "It's been so damn long since I've been to a club that I don't even remember what to expect. Hell, other than wine, I haven't had a drink in forever."

"Do you ladies need me to be your designated driver tonight? You can call me whenever you need me to pick you up."

"No, we decided we're just going to get an Uber at the end of the night. That way we're not tempted to drive and don't have to inconvenience either of our husbands."

"Oh, it wouldn't be any inconvenience, but I'd hate to be asleep and miss your call if you're out late so an Uber is probably a good idea. So I guess you're leaving your cars at home and taking an Uber there as well."

"Yep, that's the plan."

I sat back and watched as she was getting ready. She'd chosen to wear a short red dress that hugged her body perfectly. It showed a decent amount of cleavage without being overly slutty. Of course, I wouldn't have minded if slutty was the look she was going for.

"I hope you girls have a great time tonight," I said as she was putting on her heels.

"I'm sure we will. See ya when I get home!"

Kayla gave me a kiss before grabbing her purse and heading out the door to the car that was waiting for her outside.

After she left, everything was pretty much normal. I turned on the baseball game, sat down on the couch and had a couple of beers. It wasn't until she had been gone for a little over an hour that my imagination started getting the better of me.

I began to wonder about what she was doing. Was she having a good time? Was she nursing a drink while watching everyone party around her? Was she out on the dance floor with her friend? Was she grinding on any men while she was out on the dance floor? Was she flirting with anyone? Were they buying her drinks in the hopes of getting her drunk so they could get what they wanted from her?

All of these thoughts were rattling around inside my brain when one comment she'd made to me the day before came to the forefront. She had told me that her friend wanted to show her the ropes when it came to the hotwife thing.

At the time, I didn't think much of the comment, but as I sat there alone, I started wondering what that meant exactly. Was she just taking her out to show her where to meet men or was she taking her out with the intention of meeting men. I was sure that Kayla would have told me if that was the case, but it was possible that she didn't know what the plans were either.

I was no longer able to enjoy kicking back and watching the game. My mind was being far too active for that. I needed someone to talk to about what I was experiencing, but there was no way in hell that I was ever going to let my friends know about it. That's when the thought hit me. I'd go on the internet.

When I first realized I had this fantasy, I searched out information about it to make sure I wasn't crazy. As it turned out, there are lots of me who have the same fantasy as me, at least it seemed that way on the Reddit board that I found that was dedicated to the hotwife lifestyle.

Up to that point, I'd only been an observer of the threads and conversations posted. I'd never even bothered to create an account because an account wasn't necessary to read. It was time to change that. I was going to go crazy if I didn't discuss the excitement and anxiety that I was feeling with someone, so I set up an account and made my first post.

My wife is out for the first time

I've been reading the boards here for quite a while, but this is my first time making a post. About a month ago, my wife discovered that I have a wife sharing fantasy. At first, she was confused and a bit hurt that I wanted to share her, but that was because she didn't understand what the fantasy is all about.

After spending plenty of time together and having several in-depth talks, I was finally able to convince her that she is amazingly beautiful to me and that I only want to share her because she is my ultimate turn on. She turns me on far more than any porn star ever could.

This conversation led to more discussions about the fantasy and some what-if types of scenarios. We even started role-playing in bed which led to some of the best sex we've had in ages.

Fast forward to tonight and she is going out clubbing for the first time in ages. We didn't talk about her doing anything with anyone tonight, but by the way we've talked about it, I can't help but to have the thought in the back of my mind. Oh, and did I mention that she's out with a friend she hasn't seen in a while...a friend who just happens to be a hotwife herself!

Anyway, I'm not sure what I'm hoping to accomplish with this post. I guess I'm just wondering how everyone else passed the time the first time their wife went out. I've done everything I can do to occupy my mind but nothing has worked. Help!

―――――

I hit submit and figured I'd be waiting around for any replies. Of course, I figured I would get some well thought out replies from men that have been in a similar situation. It turns out that I was giving most of the guys on that particular board way too much credit. Within minutes, I had several replies, none of which were helpful at all.

————

That's really hot that your wife's out at a bar. What does she look like?

————

Where do you live? If I'm close, you can tell me what bar she's at and I can go hit on her.

————

What is your wife wearing at the club? Is she dressed like she wants to get fucked?

————

Can we see a picture of your wife? I'd love to see what she looks like naked. I bet she's fucking hot.

————

How big are your wife's tits? Does she shave her pussy?
Let's see 'em.

———

Reading the replies made me feel really sad for some of the men in the thread. Most of them were simply there hoping to score some nude pictures of people's wives. Not a single one of them were helpful to me whatsoever. If anything, it made me not want to come back to post anything else.

I put the laptop down and went for a run. Usually, I hate running, but when I want to clear my mind, it works better than anything else, even if it was just around the block a few times to work up a good sweat.

When I got home, I was going to go on Reddit and take down the post I'd made because I figured I'd just get more juvenile responses. I was surprised to see that someone had actually taken the time to send me a private message. I was even more surprised to find out that the message was sent from an actual hotwife.

———

Hi there,

I'm a hotwife and would love to offer you some insight from the woman's point of you.

I hope you don't mind me messaging you privately instead of posting in your thread. As you can see by some of the replies you've received, many of the people in here are just perverts looking for something to get them off. Anytime I post anything publicly, my inbox fills up with more dick pics than I could possibly look at.

Anyway, I wanted to write to you and let you know that what you're feeling is completely normal. According to my husband, the anxious feelings nearly made him sick to his stomach the first time I went out. He paced the house back and forth the entire time I was gone. Now, he can't wait to get that anxious feeling. He loves the way it makes him feel when he's waiting for something but isn't exactly sure what he's waiting for.

I can't speak for your wife, but if she's anything like me, she isn't going to actually do anything until you've had a conversation in which you give her explicit permission to do something. As fun as this lifestyle is, our husbands always come first, and a real hotwife won't do anything if there's even an inclination that their husband will be upset with them or if it could ruin their marriage.

I think it's cool that your wife has a friend who lives the hotwife lifestyle. That can be extremely helpful, especially if she has questions about expectations and things like that.

If she's a good hotwife, she'll explain everything to your wife, but won't push her to do anything the two of you aren't ready for.

It sounds like you and your wife have a great, loving foundation for your marriage, which is the most important thing when going into this. Just make sure she knows you love her and I guarantee she'll do the same.

If you have any questions about anything I've said or the lifestyle in general, please don't hesitate to send me a private message. I think it is good to be able to see things from both sides of the coin.

———

That one message went a long way towards putting my mind at ease. I grabbed a beer out of the fridge and was able to sit back down on the couch.

I hoped that Kayla was having a great time out at the clubs. I couldn't wait for her to get home so she could tell me all about it.

15

KAYLA

The music was loud, and the bass was pumping so hard that I could feel it in my bones. This wasn't the type of place I would have usually frequented. I was more of a hole in the wall bar type of girl, but there was no denying that everyone in the club was having a great time.

Following behind Meghann as she pushed through the sea of people heading to the bar, it was easy to see why she liked this particular club. There were men everywhere, and almost every single one of them was like a piece of eye candy. There weren't any unattractive people there at all.

I thought I'd picked a great outfit to come to the club in, but as soon as I got to Meghann's house, she looked at me and shook her head.

"What is this?" she asked.

"What is what?" I replied, genuinely confused as to what she was asking me.

"That dress is not going to work for where we're going."

"Why not? What's wrong with it?"

"We have so much work to do. Get in here."

I paid the driver and told him we weren't leaving again after all. My dress looked pretty damn sexy, at least in my opinion, so I could only imagine what Meghann had in mind for me.

She grabbed me by the hand and dragged me towards her bedroom. Along the way, we passed a tall, attractive man standing in the hallway talking on his phone.

"Hey there," he said as we walked by.

"Jack, this is Kayla. Kayla, that's my husband, Jack."

"I thought you guys were leaving."

"We are, but do you see what she's wearing? Anyway, we don't have time to talk right now, honey. I gotta get her changed so we can get out of here."

"Well, it was nice to meet you, Kayla," he laughed.

"You too," I yelled as Meghann finished pulling me into her room.

"Get out of that dress. We're gonna put you into something that's going to get you some attention."

Meghann and I were nearly the same size, so everything she had fit me perfectly. I kept pointing to different dresses she had, only to have her shake her head at me. In the end, she had me in a black dress with a pair of ankle high boots. She called them fuck me boots.

As soon as we walked up to the bar, I could feel so many eyes on me. The dress that Meghann had put on me was much shorter and lot more low cut than anything I would have ever picked out, but I was getting a hell of a lot of attention wearing it. As hard as it was to admit, it looked so good on me; I wanted to fuck myself.

We were having a great time at the club. Although I'd brought plenty of money, I didn't buy a single drink the entire night. Meghann didn't need to buy any drinks for herself either.

Even though I wasn't going to be hooking up with anyone, I knew that Meghann's husband had given her a permanent hall pass, which meant that if she wanted to sleep with someone else, she could. Armed with this knowledge, I watched how she interacted with people. If I was ever going to make my husband's fantasy come true, I needed to see how a real hotwife does things.

She spent the majority of her time out on the dance floor, dancing seductively with the men who would come up behind her. I paid attention to how she would lean in close when she whispered into their ears and how she always touched them, even if it was a minor thing.

Every single guy she came in contact with ate it up,

and before I knew it, she had multiple guys paying attention to her and basically eating out of her hands. She had drinks coming to her left and right. In fact, she had so many drinks coming her that she had to pawn some of them off on me. Not a big drinker in the first place, it didn't take long before I was feeling really good.

The alcohol allowed me to loosen up and I figured that while I was at the club, I should at least practice, just in case I decided to come out and do it for real someday.

I joined Meghann on the dance floor, and she introduced me to a couple of guys she was talking to. Before long, a couple of them had taken an interest in me and started dancing real close.

The man behind me, a tall guy with bright blue eyes, a chiseled jawline, and strong arms, grabbed me by the waist and pulled me into him. My ass was right against his crotch, and I could feel his bulge through his pants. It wasn't even hard, yet I could still feel it.

Thinking about what that could do to me started to turn me on. The man moved his hands from my hips and ran them up my body, running over my breasts and then allowing just his fingertips to run up my neck and into my hair. There was an intense lust in the air, and it was seriously making me wet. My wetness was made even worse when I felt his lips come into contact with my neck, right below my ear. He had no way of knowing this, but that was my spot.

I had no idea how long we'd been dancing, but if I didn't get away right then, I was liable to turn around and let the man fuck me right on the dance floor.

"Can you excuse me for a minute?" I asked. "I'll be right back," I told him as I made my way off the dance floor and towards the ladies rooms.

I looked around for Meghann, but she was nowhere to be found. I was dying to get her into the restroom and tell her how excited I was and see what I should do. I tried calling her from outside the bathroom door, but she didn't answer. I tried one more time and then realized I could hear her phone ringing inside the bathroom.

Relieved to know she was already inside, I opened the door and walked in, not realizing it was a bathroom intended for one person. The door had barely closed behind me before I saw Meghann, her ass barely on the edge of the sink, getting pounded by one of the men who'd been buying her shots.

I didn't mean to stare, but I couldn't believe what I was seeing. I was shocked, yet aroused. He was fucking her so hard, and I could tell that she was thoroughly enjoying herself. She glanced over and saw me standing there. Instead of getting mad and asking for privacy, she shot me a sly grin and went right back to getting fucked.

Figuring she was probably going to be a while, I went back to the dance floor and enjoyed a few more free drinks and danced with the men who were buying them for me.

Eventually, Meghann came strutting out of the restroom. Her hair was a mess, and her makeup was in shambles, but she couldn't help but flash that big bright smile at me, proud of how naughty she'd been. I had to admit that I was a bit jealous that I wasn't the one propped up on the bathroom sink getting my brains fucked out.

Before we left, the man I'd been dancing with grabbed my phone and put his number in it, telling me to call him anytime I wanted to get together, and he'd show me a great time. I said I might just have to do that, strongly considering it and wondering what Dillon would say when he found out I had another man's number in my phone.

Even though I hadn't done anything with anyone, that was never the point of going out. Meghann showed me how things were done, and even showed me how easy it was for her to hook up with someone who wanted a no-strings-attached lay. I considered the night a success and was excited for what was to come, whatever it may be.

We called our Uber and headed towards home. I couldn't wait to tell Dillon all about our night!

16

DILLON

I couldn't believe that it was actually happening. Just a week ago, my wife had gone out to a club with her friend and tonight; she was going out on a date with one of the men she'd met that night.

"Are you nervous?" I asked her as she was getting ready.

"You have no idea," she replied. "I feel like I'm gonna be sick."

"You have nothing to worry about. This is all about having fun, right?"

"Yeah, but I never thought I was going to have a first date in my life ever again. I doubt I'll even know what to do."

"I think you're overthinking things. It's not like you're trying to show the guy that you're wife material. You've already got a husband. You just want to show this guy why he wants to take you to bed."

"And then let him."

"Exactly. What are you thinking about as far as that goes? How do you feel knowing that you may sleep with someone entirely new tonight."

"I'm feeling so many things; I doubt I can describe them. It's a combination of excited, terrified, and very turned on."

"I'd say that's a good combination."

"It's exhilarating. How are you feeling?"

"I'm not sure yet. I'm definitely horny, but I'm going to wait until after your date to do anything about it. I'm nervous, but only because I've been looking at this stuff for years, so I kind of know what to expect, but I also have no idea what to expect at the same time."

Just then, her phone dinged with a text message notification.

"Oh shit, he's here to pick me up. How do I like?"

"Like a sexy wife who is begging to get fucked."

"Good, that's the look I was going for. See you later tonight."

"Have fun, babe. See you when you get home."

She kissed me on the cheek before throwing on her heels and running out the front door. She really did look like a wife wanting to get laid, and that turned me on so much. She was right about one thing. She was going to be seeing me later that night. Little did she know, she'd be seeing me much sooner than she realized.

———

"How many in your party, sir?" the restaurant hostess asked as I walked into the lobby.

"It's just me tonight, thank you."

"Okay, follow me."

The hostess led me to a table, but I was busy looking around. Finally, I spotted her across the room, sitting in a booth with her date. She looked she was having a great time.

"Ma'am, would it be okay if I sat right here?" I asked, pointing to a table directly across the room from Kayla, giving me the perfect view of her and the man who'd brought her out.

I watched intently as the hostess brought me a glass of water and a basket of bread, letting me know my waitress would be with me shortly. I wasn't even particularly hungry, but I wanted to see how the date was going.

Kayla looked breathtaking. She was glowing as she sat with the man. She was smiling and laughing. He was sitting so close to her, or maybe she was sitting close to him. Whatever it was, there was a definite chemistry, and I was glad to see it.

To the naked eye, my wife and the stranger would have appeared to be an average couple out on a date. When their food arrived, he offered her bites of his, which she accepted, eating directly off his fork.

In between bites, he would lean in and kiss her. From time to time, I'd watch as his hands disappeared beneath the table. I was surprised when her hands occasionally disappeared as well.

As their dinner was winding down, he was getting much more touchy with her, but she didn't seem to mind one bit. At one point, he was leaning into her, kissing on her neck when she looked up and saw me sitting there. I expected her eyes to get big with surprise, but they didn't. Instead, she grinned at me and kept looking me in the eyes as he groped her.

Kayla maintained eye contact as she reached down and started running her hand from his knee to his inner thigh. He matched her by putting his hand on her leg, but he didn't stop at her thigh. He kept going until his hand was all the way under her dress.

I wondered how far his hand made it, but that question was answered when Kayla made an "o" with her mouth before gently biting her bottom lip. He was touching her. Not just her body, but the most forbidden parts of her body. The parts that only I had touched for so long. I could only imagine how wet she was.

He pulled his hand out from under her dress and excused himself to go to the restroom. As soon as he was out of sight, I threw cash on the table to pay for my food and went right over to their table.

"I need you to come with me," I told her.

Kayla didn't question anything. She simply took me by the hand, slid out of the booth, and followed me towards the front door. The other patrons in the restaurant were whispering to one another since she had just been there with another man, but we didn't care. There was only one thing on our minds.

I led her to our car, which I'd parked in the very back corner of the parking lot. Without saying a word, I opened the back door, pushed her in front of me, and grabbed her dress by the bottom, lifting it up above her waist.

She pressed her back against my chest, and I leaned in to kiss her. The kiss was sexy, deep, and full of wanting. I couldn't control myself any longer.

Using plenty of force, I bent her over the back seat of the car and pulled her panties to the side, revealing her beautiful, glistening pussy. It was freshly shaved, so she was prepared for anything happening.

With one hand, I unzipped my pants and unleashed my cock, which was hard and already throbbing. There was no foreplay required. We were both ready to go. Grabbing her hips, I pushed myself into her. She was so wet that I slid in without any resistance.

There was a thrill to knowing that we could be caught at any moment, and I wondered what her date would think if he came out looking for her, only to find her getting pounded in the back seat of the car. It didn't matter, I had to have her, and I couldn't wait.

This was no lovemaking session. I was moving in and out of her hard and fast. She made attempts to stifle her moans, but her efforts were not working. I wanted to hear her. I gave her ass a firm slap as I pounded into her, leading her to let out a yelp, which was part pain and part pleasure.

I reached around her and started playing with her clit, knowing that would do her in. Almost instantly, her legs became shaky, and her pussy tightened around me.

"Fuck Dillon, I'm cumming."

Grabbing a handful of her hair, I starting pumping into her as hard and fast as I could. If anyone had been walking to their cars, there was no way they could have avoided hearing the sounds of my pelvis smacking against her ass.

I had to bite my tongue as I exploded inside of my wife, both of us reaching orgasm at the same time.

"Fuck," she whimpered as I pushed myself all the way

inside of her, bent down, and kissed her just below the neck.

"Fuck is right," I replied. "That was fucking amazing."

"That was fucking hot is what that was."

"Let me find something for you to wipe up with."

"No, I'm not wiping up. I want to go home knowing you're inside of me."

She stood up, slid her panties back into position, turned and kissed me.

"So, you want to go back in and finish your date?"

"No, I just want to go home with you."

17

KAYLA

Although I still hadn't slept with anyone else, the experience I'd had on the date I went had left me with a ton of confidence. The ending of the date with Dillon was a huge bonus as well.

Needless to say, the gentleman I'd gone out with wasn't too amused with the fact that I left him alone inside the restaurant, especially considering how much we'd been teasing each other. I tried to explain to him what had happened, but he didn't want to hear it. The man had planned on getting laid, and I left him with blue balls.

When I told Meghann the story, I thought she was going to die of laughter. That was one hotwife experience that she hadn't been able to enjoy yet. In fact, she yelled at her husband when I told her and asked him why he's never done that. Apparently, it's being planned.

Since the original man wasn't willing to give me a second date, Meghann offered to help me out. She had a client at work that was always looking for female company when he was in town. She told me that he was older, but that he didn't look or act his age. The best part, according to her, was the fact that he had more money that he knew what to do with and he loved spending money on his dates. Money has never been a big thing to me, but if someone wanted to buy me a couple of gifts for me as part of our date, who was I to argue? I told her to go ahead and set it up.

His name was Jeff, and we spoke on the phone a few times to make sure we liked each other's personalities and to get an overall feel for each other. He seemed like a nice enough guy, and I didn't pick up on any red flags, so we went ahead and set up a date.

Since he only came into town a few times a year, he wanted to make a day out of it. Dillon was working so he wasn't able to see me off, but that was okay. I liked knowing that he would be at work all day, wondering exactly what I was doing while I was out.

My jaw dropped open when a full-sized limousine pulled out in front of my house. I knew the guy had money, but I had no clue it was going to be so on display. I was glad that all of our neighbors worked during the day or else I may have had a bunch of questions to answer, especially considering how nosy all of my neighbors are.

I found it odd that Jeff didn't come to the door to get me, instead of sending his driver to let me know they had arrived. Figuring that was probably just the life he was used to, I didn't think much of it.

The driver held the door open for me, and I slid in, laying eyes on Jeff for the first time. Meghann was right. The man looked far younger than his age, which I found to be a relief. There's nothing wrong with an older man, as long as he aged well, but too many men fail to do that. Fortunately for me, this one had aged as gracefully as George Clooney.

Aside from his appearance, the first thing I noticed was his scent. A familiar smell greeted me as I sat across from him. A scent that I would recognize anywhere. He was wearing Polo Blue, the same cologne that my husband wears. I guess the other half doesn't live that different after all.

"Wow, you look beautiful," he said as I positioned myself in the seat.

"You're not so bad yourself," I replied with a wink.

"Would you like a drink?"

"No thanks, it's still early for me, or are you just trying to get me drunk so you can take advantage of me?"

"Oh, I don't think I have to get you drunk to make that happen."

There was something about the way those words came out of his mouth. I couldn't put my finger on it, but they didn't sit right with me for some reason.

"So what are the plans for the day?" I asked, hoping to get the conversation moving in a different direction.

"I've got some ideas, but what we do all depends on you."

"On me? What does that mean?"

"Let's just say, the happier you make me, the happier you'll be with today's activities."

He slid out of his seat and came over to sit next to me. Almost immediately, he had his hand on my leg and his lips on my neck. I tried to play it cool, but his aggressiveness was making me uncomfortable.

"Whoa, let's slow it down a little bit. There will be plenty of time for that later," I told him, throwing in a little laugh so it wouldn't sound so harsh.

"I'm not a take it slow kind of guy. I live my life with the pedal to the metal."

"There's nothing wrong with that, but I'd like to get to know you a little bit first."

"That's fine. Driver, take us to Cafe Sebastienne."

"Cafe Sebastienne? I've never been there."

"It's a cool little lunch spot. I know the owner so we'll

be well taken care of," he announced, moving back to his seat.

The ride to the restaurant was pretty quiet. It was clear that he was a man who didn't like to be told no. I worried that maybe I came off too mean. After all, the whole purpose of being a hotwife is to have sex with other men. Still, I don't think it was asking too much to be respected.

Being the type of girl who will go to a sports bar and order chicken wings, so to food at this restaurant was a little eclectic for my tastes. Not knowing what most of the menu was, I opted for the fish tacos while Jeff ordered something with goat cheese. The food was decent, but not worth anything near the price tag.

As soon as we got back into the limo, he started eyeballing me and sizing me up. I tried making small talk and asked what was up next, but he ignored what I was saying. Instead, he kept creeping closer and closer to me until I was pinned against the closed door.

Jeff grabbed me by my hair and started kissing me roughly. There wasn't even any warm up. He just kept shoving his tongue into my mouth. I tried pushing him away, but he put his weight on me to hold me in place. After a few minutes, I was able to put a bit of distance between us, at least enough so that I was able to get his mouth off of mine.

"Jeff, what are you doing?"

"What does it look like I'm doing. I'm about to fuck you."

"This isn't the way you go about it."

"What do you mean? You're a hotwife, right? I just bought you a meal; now you're going to give me my dessert."

"What the fuck? You think I'm so kind of cheap slut?"

"Well, yeah. What kind of woman would sleep with men other than their husband if they weren't a slut?"

"Wow, okay, we're done here. Take me home please."

"I'll get you back when we're done. Don't worry. Besides, with that attitude, I don't want to spend any extra time with you if I don't have to."

He went back to kissing me while pulling my dress down, exposing my breasts. Jeff was so strong and pinned me to the door, making it very hard for me to move. He was groping me like I was a piece of property instead of a woman.

After a lot of maneuvering and wiggling, I got my right arm free and was able to reach down into my purse and grab the mace that Dillon has insisted I buy if I were going to go on these dates. I told him he was being ridiculous, but he refused to back down. I was very grateful for him at that moment.

I pulled the mace out of my purse, put it right in front

of his face, shielded my eyes, and pushed down, sending a pungent spray straight into his eyes.

As quickly as he pounced on me, he slithered back to his side of the seat.

"What the fuck? You maced me, you stupid slutty bitch!"

I didn't wait around to see what else he had to say. I opened the door, jumped out, put my breasts away, and ran back into the restaurant.

"Can I help you?" the host asked, sensing that I was upset or in trouble.

"Where is your bathroom?" I began to cry.

Inside the bathroom, I brought up the Uber app and set up a ride home. My driver would arrive in about 10 minutes. I also called Dillon, who had just gotten home and told him that I was on my way.

I was so happy when the driver pulled up in front of my house. It was truly my safe place, my happy place, and I just wanted to be inside with my husband.

After paying for the ride, I ran into the house, slammed through the door, and jumped into Dillon's arms. I'd planned to stay strong, but I couldn't help but break down. My cries quickly turned to sobs.

"I don't want to do this anymore."

18

DILLON

In the entirety of our marriage, I'd never seen Kayla break down like that. She was a tough girl. I'd barely even seen her cry.

"What's wrong Kayla? What happened?"

"That man! He was such a creep," she said between sobs. "He wouldn't take no for an answer.

"Did he do something you didn't want him to do?"

"He tried. I kept telling him no, but he wouldn't listen. At first, he stopped, but after he took me to lunch, he was right back to being all over me. I kept saying no and he basically said I owed him because he took me to lunch. He wouldn't stop, so I maced him."

"I'm so sorry babe, wait a minute, you maced him?" I asked, making sure I heard her correctly.

"Yeah, I sprayed him with the mace you bought me."

We sat in silence for a few moments before I looked down at her and we both started to laugh.

"I can't believe you maced someone. That's awesome."

"He had it coming, babe. He might have all the money in the world, but when a woman says no, she means it."

"Creeps like that don't deserve to be with a wife as awesome as you. What did he do when you maced him?"

"Well, first of all, he backed the fuck up really quick. Then he just started screaming. You bitch! You fucking bitch! I don't know what he said after that because I booked it out of there and called for a ride home."

"Why didn't you call me? I would have come and picked you up."

"I don't know. I wasn't sure if you were still working and I didn't want to inconvenience you."

"Sweetheart, you are never an inconvenience. Don't even have that thought in your head, okay?"

"All right, anyway, I hope you won't be mad at me, but I really don't want to do this anymore. Maybe someday we can explore things again, but this was a really scary experience and it could have gone way worse than it did."

"Oh baby, I'm not going to be mad at you. Your safety has always been my priority. If you don't want to do this anymore, you don't have to."

I'd be lying if I said I wasn't at least a little disappointed that the full fantasy wasn't ever going to happen.

Still, the fantasy would take a backseat to my wife's happiness. Alway. There were no exceptions to that rule whatsoever.

"Thanks babe."

"You know it," I said, kissing her gently on her forehead. "You know, we've been role-playing this for a while. I've really enjoyed that. What would think about still doing that with me?"

"I've had so much fun role-playing with you. There's no way in hell I'm giving that up. I'll still play into your fantasies, I love it."

I held her in my arms the entire night. I knew it wouldn't make the bad the things that happened go away, but I hoped I could at least console her and make her feel safe.

The next morning, I had to get up early because I was headed to Chicago for the annual medical conference. The conference is a huge three-day event where we get to learn all about the latest medical advances and every pharmaceutical rep on the planet tries to sell us on their latest treatments and medication.

The sun wasn't even close to being up and Kayla was sleeping peacefully. I didn't want to wake her up, especially after the long night she had, so I gave her a kiss on the cheek and crept out of the room. I left her a not before leaving.

Kayla,

You looked like an angel sleeping and I didn't want to wake you up. I just wanted to tell you that I love you and when I get back, I'm going to plan a special night for us. You can call me anytime. If I'm listening to a speaker or something, just leave a message and I'll call you right back. Can't wait to be back home to you. I love you.

Dillon

19

KAYLA

It was strange having my weekday night off without Dillon home. Since we've been working on things, I'm used to having him with me on my days off.

I had planned to get up so I could see him off to his trip, but I must have been so exhausted. Still, I was a bit disappointed to wake up and not find him lying next to me. At least he made me smile with the note he left me.

Looking at the clock, I could see that he should have been boarding his plane. Of course, his flights are always delayed. That was the type of luck he had when taking trips. I can't think of one single instance when he's had a flight leave at its scheduled time. Instead of calling him, I decided to send him a text, just in case his phone was off.

Good morning handsome, hope you have a great flight. Call me when you get there. Love you so much. -K

Still very tired from all the crying I'd done, I needed some coffee to wake me up. I smiled a huge smile when I walked into the kitchen and saw that he'd already brewed a pot for me. It was a full pot, too, which meant that he stopped for some shitty gas station coffee for himself so that I wouldn't have to go through the trouble of making any. This was the man I'd been missing for so many years.

When Dillon had convinced me to get into the whole hotwife thing, I set up profiles at several different dating sites. Well, casual sex sites would be a better way to describe them, cause you're not going to find your soulmate there.

One by one, I closed each account, checking out the messages one last time before I did so. I was the type to reply to every single message, even if I wasn't interested at all. I figured if I messaged someone, I wouldn't want to be waiting around for a reply if they weren't into it. Dillon thought it was ridiculous, especially considering the number of responses I received, but I couldn't help it.

I had been on a total of four websites, and after a little over an hour, I finally made it to the final site. There was always the least number of messages on that particular site, mostly because the company does a full vetting process to make sure that no psychopaths or serial killers made their way on there.

For the entire time I'd been on the site, I'd only received two messages, one of which had come from someone who worked for the company and the other was a gentleman who was simply too far away to be practical. Surprisingly, there was a one over the envelope at the top corner of the screen indication that I had a message. I clicked on it to see what it said.

Hey there!

My name is Kevin, and I'm a professional male in my mid-30s. I know this sounds strange, but I was just browsing the website and seeing what it was all about. I didn't plan on messaging anyone, but as soon as I came across your ad, I knew I had to get verified so I could speak with you.

Anyway, I just wanted to let you know that you are one of the most beautiful women I've ever seen. Your eyes are mesmerizing, and your smile is amazing. I see that you're married and while that's not something I've ever done before, I would like the chance to get to know you.

As for myself, I have never been married and have no kids. I work a lot and have just never really had time for relationships. I am a very sexual person, but more than that, I am a gentleman. I'm polite, respectful and never pushy. If you're still looking for someone to play with, I'd love to be considered. Just send me a message and let me know.

Hopefully I'll talk to you soon.

For some reason, I couldn't make myself delete the message. There was something about it that spoke to me. Instead of trashing it right away, I decided to go check out his pictures.

He was attractive. Certainly heads and tails above most of the men who had messaged me on the other websites. He was well dressed and had gentle eyes, a quality I admire. In many ways, this man reminded me a lot of Dillon, which in all honesty, I've looked for in potential partners.

His profile matched what he had said in his message. He was a professional man who works way too many hours and misses the touch of a woman. Again, it said he was respectful and not aggressive, which sounded great after what I had been through.

Intrigued, I sent a message, unsure of when he would reply, if he ever did. These websites were notorious for men that would sign up, send some messages, and then never get back on. A part of me hoped he would reply.

Much to my surprise, a response came back almost instantly. He said he was working and didn't have much time to chat, but if we wanted, we could send messages back and forth, and he'd reply when he could.

That sounded good to me so I posted a response letting him know that I would love to get to know him that way. Something told me that he was a good guy, so I decided to give him a chance. A little conversation never hurt anyone.

Throughout the day, we messaged back and forth, and he did a great job putting me at ease that he wasn't anything like the man I'd met the day previously. I'm still not completely sure how it happened, but by the time he was leaving the office, we were making plans for what time he was going to pick me up.

———

This man was the complete opposite of the creep in the limo. Kevin was a perfect gentleman. Even though he knew exactly what my situation was, it didn't stop him from treating me in the same way that he'd treat someone he was dating seriously. Sure, the goal was to get into my pants, but he didn't act like it.

We had an amazing date. First, he took me to a cool little sports bar downtown with a light, fun atmosphere. He attempted to teach me how to play darts, which I discovered I was terrible at. Surprisingly, I did even worse when it came to air hockey, but I still had a good time.

After dinner, we went dancing and a club far smaller than the one Meghann took me to, which wasn't necessarily a bad thing. Again, the vibe was calm and relaxed, which helped keep me comfortable.

The flirting between Kevin and I increased as the night went on. The more comfortable he made me feel, the more suggestive my flirting became. Our dancing was downright graphic by the time the night was over.

"I hope you had a great time," he said as he walked me outside to wait for my ride.

Instead of answering, I stood on my toes, wrapped my arms around his neck and gave him a huge kiss before pulling him into me so I could whisper into his ear.

"Why don't you come home with me?"

20

DILLON

Traveling always wears me out, so I was sleeping soundly and deeply when my cell phone started to ring in the middle of the night. Rubbing my eyes, I attempted to focus on the clock sitting next to the bed. It was 2:21 am, and I wondered who would be calling me.

When I picked up my phone up to answer it, I was surprised to see that it wasn't a voice call. Instead, it was a FaceTime video call from Kayla. I figured she must be missing me and since she works so late, her schedule is a little messed up, and she might just be getting ready to go to bed.

I accepted the call, but I wasn't prepared for what appeared on the screen in front of me. Kayla was in our bed, on all fours, looking into the camera while someone was fucking her from behind.

"Hi, honey," eventually managed to escape her lips between moans and grunts.

I had no idea who the man was, and I didn't care. I was instantly turned on by what I was watching. In my fantasies, I always imagined that she would send me text updates while she was out and maybe a picture or a video clip here or there or that I would be watching her in person. I never even thought about sharing the experience over a video call.

"Do you like what you're seeing, baby? Is this what you wanted?"

"You are so fucking sexy," I told her while I slid my free hand under the blankets to grab my cock, which had turned hard instantly the minute the video popped up.

She propped the phone up on the table while she rolled onto her back and the mystery man climbed on top of her. Watching as he grabbed her legs, put them on his shoulders, and slid inside of her caused me to start stroking myself faster.

Seeing his cock disappearing into my wife was driving me inside. My body was beginning to shake, but not because I was upset. I was shaking because I was so excited

"Oh my God Dillon, this cock feels so good! Do you see what he's doing to me? Fuck me, Mark! Fuck me harder!"

He did as she asked and started pounding into her. I heard her familiar moans, the ones that start to change just a bit as she got close to orgasm. I decided I wanted to participate.

"Go ahead, Kayla. Cum all over his cock. Let me hear it."

He reached down and started playing with her clit while he pumped himself in and out of her. I could see her body tensing up as an orgasm ripped through her body.

Hearing her getting louder and louder as she came was too much for me to handle. I ripped the blankets back and jerked myself quickly, making myself cum at almost the same time she did. My orgasm may have been just as intense as hers.

Getting off didn't do anything to my erection, which remained hard and stiff while the man continued to plow into my wife. I grabbed a hand towel that was near the bed and wiped off before I went right back to stroking myself.

I watched as this guy enjoyed Kayla's pussy, my pussy. I knew how good that pussy felt and I wished I was in his place right then and there.

He started to moan and move faster, telling her that he was going to cum. My eyes widened as Kayla squeezed her tits together and looked him right in the eyes.

"Cum for me, baby. Cum all over my tits."

He pulled out, maneuvered himself up my wife's body and stroked himself as he came all over her chest. My eyes rolled into the back of my head as I started getting off again as well. What I was watching was better than the best porn ever made.

He bent down and kissed her before she turned to the phone.

"I love you, baby," she told me, blowing a kiss into the phone before ending the FaceTime session.

I was left breathless. It didn't even seem real. It was easily the most exciting thing I had ever experienced. I officially had a hotwife.

21

KAYLA

My brain felt like it was scrambled. It was trying to think of a million different things, but couldn't think of anything at all. The only thought that could get through was holy fuck; I actually did it! I actually fucked another man. Not only that, but my husband got to watch the whole thing take place.

I couldn't believe that I'd actually gone through with it. I knew that was always the plan when I actively started seeking out men, but I always questioned whether or not I could actually do it when it came down to it.

Calling Dillon on FaceTime wasn't something either he or I had ever discussed. It was just a spur of the moment decision I had when I grabbed my phone to send him some photos. I wanted to find a good way to include him, even though he wasn't there.

Kevin left shortly after we were done, but I was still lying in bed. Each time I closed my eyes, I could see Dillon's face as he answered the video call. His eyes got so big, and his mouth dropped open. I'd been worried that he would be mad, but when I saw him relax in his bed and whip his dick out, I knew he was probably going to be okay.

Even though it had just happened, it still didn't seem real. I felt so sexually liberated and was still incredibly turned on. I just laid there on the bed, rubbing my clit with my fingers, letting orgasm after orgasm take me away to bliss.

Something was missing, though. I'd included my husband in the act of me becoming his hotwife, but now I was all alone. I always figured that if I actually had sex with another man, Dillon would be there afterward to love me and let me know that I still belonged to him. I didn't have that, and it made me sad.

I laid down on the bed and brought his pillows in close to me. If he couldn't be here to cuddle me, I was going to cuddle his pillows instead. I inhaled deeply, taking in his scent which lingered behind.

Since I couldn't have him with me, I at least wanted to hear his voice. I wanted to know what he thought about what he saw and if it was everything he'd hoped it would be. Still holding his pillows tightly, I grabbed my phone and called my husband.

22

DILLON

Once the FaceTime video was turned off, I laid in bed for a few minutes attempting to process what I had just watched. There were so many feelings and emotions fighting within me that I didn't even know what most of them were. It didn't matter. The excitement was winning out over all of them.

There was no way I was going to be able to sleep for the rest of the night. Not after what had just happened. I jumped out of bed, grabbed my suitcase and started throwing things into it as fast as I could. It would have driven Kayla nuts to see how I was tossing things in there unfolded and in no particular order. Having things neat and orderly was one of her quirks, and I could almost hear her nagging at me for the way things looked in my bag.

I made one last sweep of the room and the bathroom

to make sure I didn't forget anything before I wheeled my suitcase out of the room and down to the front desk.

"Could you call me a cab to the airport?" I asked, still wiping the sleep from my eyes.

"Absolutely, sir. If you would like some coffee, we have some in the lobby there."

Typically, I needed coffee to wake myself up, but it wasn't necessary that morning. The video call was plenty to get my blood pumping and have me ready to go.

I walked outside to wait for the cab and quickly remembered why they called Chicago the windy city. The air attempted to bite through me until I found a spot meant for smokers on the side of the front doors.

The medical conference that I was in town for quickly became an afterthought. I loved the conference, but I didn't care about missing this one. I'd been a speaker during previous years, but not this one, so nobody was going to miss me. People may look for me, but with the sheer number of medical professionals that would be there, it's impossible to meet up with everyone.

Another added plus was the fact that a recap is also posted on the internet so that doctors who weren't able to make it can learn about anything important that happened. The recap always included new products, treatments, and medications so if there was something that interested me; I'd be able to reach out to the company directly.

I didn't care about the conference; I didn't care about the fact that I'd prepaid for my room, I didn't care about anything other than getting home to my wife.

After what seemed like forever, the cab finally arrived to take me to the airport. I probably should have called the airport to see if there were any flights going out and if there were, if there was even a spot on one so I could get home.

As my luck would have it, there was traffic at 3:30 am. Apparently, the city had started work on a bridge and had the four-lane highway down to one in each direction. I was tempted to get out and walk to the airport, sure that it would be faster.

The cab finally pulled up to the airport just before 4:00 in the morning, and tossed the driver some cash, grabbed my suitcase and ran straight to the ticketing desk.

"Hi, do you have anything going to Kansas City?"

"Yes sir, we have a flight leaving in about 15 minutes. It's all the way down at gate 19, so you'd have to hurry. We also have one leaving at 7:15 am. Which would you prefer?"

"I'll take the one leaving in 15 minutes."

I gave the ticketing agent all of my information, got my ticket and boarding pass and took off as fast as I could.

I was fortunate that there wasn't a line for security and they didn't stop me for a random check. I was completely out of breath but made it to the terminal just as they were announcing the last call for passengers.

The plane was not overcrowded, which I was thankful for. On the flight to Chicago, we were pinned in like sardines, so it was nice to have the row of seats to myself.

Once I was on the flight, I was finally able to sit down and process everything that had happened. I was surprised by all of the emotions I was beginning to feel. They were all over the place, with lots of highs and lows.

The emotion that surprised me the most was the jealousy. I was very jealous that another man had just been with my wife. It was a jealousy that I could feel deep within the pit of my stomach. The funny thing about it was that it wasn't the typical jealousy that someone would feel. It wasn't a bad feeling.

I actually liked the jealous feeling that I had and know that I want the whole thing to happen again. The sense of jealousy and angst were like a drug, and I knew that all it took was one hit to become addicted.

The best part about the experience was the fact that it was unexpected. When Kayla was going out before, I knew there was a chance that something could happen. This experience came as a total surprise. The last I knew, she was done with the whole thing. Receiving that call from her was the last thing I ever would have expected. The surprise element was definitely what turned me on the most.

As I'm sitting in my seat, my cell phone begins to ring. It was Kayla. I had to fight with myself not to answer the call. I wanted to talk to her so bad so we could discuss what had happened. I also wanted to know how the experience was from her end. Regardless of how bad I wanted to answer the call, I allowed it to go to voicemail. I wanted the fact that I was on my way home to her to be a surprise.

23

KAYLA

Why wasn't Dillon answering his phone? I called him several times and each time got the same result. It would ring four times before going to his voicemail. Something wasn't right, and I didn't like it.

I paced around the house wondering whether or not I'd made a mistake. I knew what room he was in, so I called the hotel and asked to be transferred. The phone just rang and rang. Dillon is an incredibly light sleeper, so there was no way he had gone back to bed and was sleeping through his phone ringing. Besides, how could he sleep after all of that? I had so much adrenaline flowing through my veins and knew he had to have the same feeling as well.

He couldn't be mad at me, could he? This whole thing

had been his idea, so it wouldn't be fair to me if he were pissed off that I'd gone through with it.

There was always the possibility that he was upset because I did it behind his back. He always knew when I was out on dates and things like that, so maybe he didn't like the fact that he wasn't kept in the loop. If that was the case, I could understand it, but I thought that doing it the way I did would make him happy.

I was looking directly into his eyes when we were on our FaceTime call. He didn't look mad then. There wasn't even a hint of anger in his eyes. I saw excitement, but there was nothing that would have told me he was mad.

Frustration was starting to get the best of me, and I was getting worried that I'd messed everything up. I needed to talk to him, and I didn't care how many times I had to call. I was going to blow his phone up until he answered me. If I had pissed him off, I deserved to hear him say it instead of giving me the silent treatment. I grabbed my phone and dialed his number.

DILLON

My phone was ringing as I walked into the front door. As

I closed it behind me, I heard footsteps running in my direction.

"Dillon! What the hell?" Kayla yelled as she came running towards me, throwing her arms around me and kissing me before she punched me in the arm.

"What was that for?" I asked, playfully rubbing my arm as though the punch had hurt me.

"Do you have any idea how many times I've called you?"

"I figured you've probably been calling a lot. I had to turn my phone off during the flight, so I probably missed most of them."

"Why in the hell are you here? You have that whole conference in front of you. Are you flying back in the morning?"

"No, I'm going to skip the conference this year."

"Can you do that?"

"Of course I can do that. It's not like there's some requirement that says you lose your license to practice medicine unless you attend every medical conference, I laughed. "Besides, I'm right where I need to be right now."

Kayla wrapped her arms around me again, burying her head in my chest.

"You know I love you, right?" she asked, looking up at me with big, beautiful puppy dog eyes.

"I love you too. That's why I'm here."

"Don't ever make me think that you're mad at me again, especially after something like that."

"I'm sorry, babe. I didn't want you to think I was mad at you. I just didn't want you to know I was coming home. I wanted to surprise."

"You surprised me after giving me anxiety all night."

"Come here," I tell her as I hug her again and kiss her on her forehead. "I didn't mean to leave you wondering. I just wanted to see the excitement on your face when I got home. I love you so very much, and I could never tell you that enough."

"I love you too, Dillon."

"I can't believe you did it."

"I know, I'm still in shock myself."

"What happened to not wanting to do it anymore?"

"Oh, I came across a guy who was the exact opposite of the asshole that wouldn't take no for an answer. He was polite and respectful and was more than willing to put on a show for you."

"I was so surprised when I picked up my phone."

"You should have seen your face. I thought your jaw was going to hit the floor."

"Just so you know, it was fucking hot."

"Yeah? You should have been on my end of it," she laughed.

"You know that the experience is not completely over for you, right?"

"What do you mean?" she asked with a look of genuine confusion on her face.

"I'm not here just because I wanted to see you. I'm here because I need to reclaim you. I'm here because I couldn't wait to take back what's mine. Come with me."

I stood up, grabbed her hand, lifted her from the couch and led her to the bedroom.

24

KAYLA

In all the years that we've been married, I had never seen that look in his eyes. It was a look of hunger and desire, and while I know that he's desired me plenty in the past, this look was different. There was a fire behind them that I don't think I'd ever seen before then.

When he grabbed my hand and pulled me off the couch, I could feel an electricity in his touch. As we walked to the bedroom, he pulled me in front of me and gave me a hard swat on my ass. I yelped, but I loved it. I've always wanted him to be more physically dominant with me, and that was one hell of a good start.

As soon as we got into the bedroom, he grabbed me by the face and kissed me harder than he'd ever kissed me before. It was the kind of kiss you'd give someone if you'd been apart for a year and are seeing each other again for the first time.

Releasing his lips from mine, Dillon grabbed me by the back of my head and pushed me down onto my knees. Up until that point, he wasn't saying anything to me. He didn't have to. He was maneuvering me into whatever position he wanted me in, and I was more than happy to follow his lead.

Positioned where he wanted me, he slid off his pants, grabbed another handful of my hair and shoved his already stiff cock into my mouth. I started to move my mouth back and forth on it, but he stopped me. Instead, he held my head still and fucked my mouth.

I was amazed by the aggressiveness he was showing. I didn't think he had it in him, but it was hot. Over and over, he plunged his thick dick into the back of my throat while I fought my gag reflexes with all I had. At one point, I couldn't help but gag, and he responded by pushing his cock even deeper into my throat.

"Did he go down on you?"

"What?" I asked, not sure I heard him correctly.

Dillon pulled his dick out of my mouth.

"Did he lick your pussy?"

"Yes."

"Did he make you cum while he licked your pussy?"

"No."

"Amateur."

He lifted me off the floor, kissed me hard again, and then threw me down onto the bed. He raised the lace nightgown I was wearing, pulled my panties to the side and buried his head between my legs.

My eyes rolled into the back of my head almost instantly as his tongue started lapping up all of my juices. There was something incredibly erotic about the fact that my husband had his tongue exactly where another man had been earlier in the evening.

He used one hand to spread my lips apart while the other was used to slide two fingers inside of me. Up and down and side to side, his tongue moved in a constant motion while he slowly began to move those fingers in and out of my tight hole.

Kevin was pretty damn good when it came to oral, but I doubted anyone would ever be able to compare to Dillon. He knew the right spots to touch and the exact ways to touch me. His tongue knew exactly how to move to make me feel good.

I started to moan and grabbed a handful of my husband's hair. Dillon knew exactly what that meant. He was aware that hair grab meant I was getting close. He also knew exactly what to do to put me over the edge.

Using the hand that had been spreading my lips, he lubricated his middle finger with my wetness and slid it right into my ass. The new sensation brought me right to the brink, so Dillon curled his fingers inside my tight hole, pressing directly against my g-spot.

That was all it took for me to lose control. My legs began to shake, and my moaning turned into loud screams of pleasure.

"Fuck, Dillon! I'm going to cum all over your face."

The curling of his fingers continued as he pushed up against my g-spot more and more. My hips rolled involuntarily as I threw my head back and let the sensations take over my body.

I came for what felt like forever. Every time I thought I was done, Dillon would press up with his fingers again, sending another wave of orgasms through my body. Even as I started to become sensitive, he wouldn't stop. He only stopped when he decided I had had enough.

Once he slid his fingers out of my pussy, he climbed on top of me and kissed me. This was a change as he never kissed me after oral and I loved it. I could smell myself on him, and I enjoyed the way I tasted on his lips and his tongue.

From out of nowhere, he grabbed me around the outside of my thighs and yanked me forcefully to the edge of the bed.

"Now it's time to take back what belongs to me," he told me in a stern tone.

The tone of his voice was one that I had never heard him use before. It was demanding and dominating. More than anything else, it was hot as hell.

Positioned on the edge of the bed just how he wanted me, he spread my thighs apart and pushed himself into me. I moaned out in surprise because, again, it was out of character for him. He usually did things like rubbing his head on my clit and teasing before he slowly entered me inch by inch. Instead, he pushed himself all the way into me, nearly taking my breath away.

"Who's pussy is this?" he asked.

"It's yours, Dillon," I moaned.

"I said who does this pussy belong to?" he demanded, pounding into me harder.

"It's yours, Dillon. This pussy belongs to you!"

It only took a couple of minutes before I was coming again. I tried to wrap my arms around him, so I could pull him into me and kiss him. It's something I love to do when I'm getting off, but he wasn't having any of it. Instead, he reached down and started playing with my clit.

"You wanted to be a slut, right? Isn't this what a little slut likes?"

"Yes, sir," I moaned, surprised by what I had said.

"Sir? Yeah, I like that. You can fucking call me sir! Now, is the little slut going to cum for me?"

"Oh God, yes!"

"Yes, what?"

"Oh fuck! Yes, yes, sir! I'm coming, sir!"

What followed was easily the hardest, most intense orgasm I'd ever experienced up to that point. At one point, I even scared myself because it felt like I couldn't get a breath. He kept sliding in and out me, pressing upward on my clit to ensure that my orgasm kept rolling. I felt like it was never going to stop, and I wasn't sure I ever wanted it to.

Eventually, I came down from my Dillon-induced high, and he ordered me to get on all fours. Positioning himself behind me, he grabbed my hips and slammed his throbbing cock into my hole, which had been dripping since this all started.

"Was this how you were getting fucked when you called me?"

"Yes!"

A hard slap came down on my ass.

"I asked if this was how you were getting fucked when you called me?"

"Yes! This is how I was getting fucked when you called me."

Another hard smack, this time on my other ass cheek. This one was harder and stung quite a bit, yet I loved it much more than the first.

"I'm only going to ask you this one more time, and you

better answer correctly. Is this how you were getting fucked when you called me?"

"Yes, sir!" I shouted out, remembering the order he had given me earlier.

"Good, now let me show you how it should be done."

He pounded into me hard and fast, smacking my ass here and there, catching me off guard and making me yell out in a mixture of pain and pleasure.

He had never fucked me like that. Not even close. He was the type that always liked it soft, sweet, and sensual. While that is nice, there are times when a girl just wants her brains fucked out, and that's what he was giving me. It was animalistic and territorial. It was as though seeing me with someone had set something off in him and he had to remind me who I belonged to.

Dillon was never in danger of losing me to the other man, and I'm pretty sure he knew it as well, but this was something evolutionary. It was like the experience triggered something within him that said he had to show an act of aggression to show who the real man was. I was happy to oblige him.

He pounded me so hard that at one point, the only sounds you could hear was my screaming and his balls smacking against my clit, echoing on the walls around us. I'd never had so many orgasms in one sex session as I did with him. He had unbelievable stamina. While he had never been a two pump chump, a good ten minutes was what I knew I could expect from him. Looking at the lock, he'd been fucking me hard for close to an hour.

I knew he wasn't going to be able to hold out much longer as soon as he pushed me down flat on my stomach, his cock remaining deep inside of me. Dillon wrapped his arms around my waist, holding me tightly while pushing into me as deep as he could.

"Tell me you want me to cum!" he ordered.

"I want you to cum, sir!"

"You want me to fill that pussy up, don't you?"

"Yes, sir. Fill me up."

"Oh my God, Kayla, I'm going to cum!"

"Cum for me, sir."

"Oh fuck, Kayla! I love you so much!"

I could feel him beginning to throb and swell inside of me, which was something I'd never been able to feel before. Gripping the sheets, I wanted to feel him exploding inside of me, yet I didn't want this experience to end. I wanted to continue feeling him inside of me while he made me his again.

He fucked me senseless for about another minute until he pushed deep into me and pumped me full of the biggest load he'd ever given me. I could feel the head of his cock pulsating as he unleashed himself into my wanting pussy, making us one.

Just like that, we were whole again. Just like that, he had fucked the other man out of me and made me his. When he was done, he rolled over and maneuvered his head to his pillows.

"Come here, sweetheart," he whispered.

I slithered over to him, allowing him to pull me tightly into him. With his arm wrapped around me, I laid my head on his chest. A smile remained on my face until I eventually drifted off to sleep, Dillon leaking out of me. It was the best night ever.

25

DILLON

I was surprised by how quickly our lives were able to go back to normal after our first hotwife experience. The sex that we had that night was intense and was honestly the best sex we've ever had, which was something I didn't know how to feel about.

There were a lot of emotions and feelings afterward that were difficult to deal with. These feelings surprised me. There was jealousy and questioning whether or not I'd made the right decision to ever bring it up. Through some research, I'd learned that these feeling were all very normal and as long as communication was good, they'd pass as quickly as they came, which is exactly what happened.

In the two weeks that followed our experience, Kayla and I have talked a lot about what went down and what we enjoyed most about it. I obviously liked watching the pleasure on her face, and she enjoyed the different experience. We both agreed that my reclaiming her was our favorite part of all.

We continued to do a lot of role-playing in bed. She talked dirty about the things other men could do to her, and I'd tell her what a dirty slut she was. It was always very erotic.

There was one thing that didn't come up in these conversations, however. She never brought up doing it again. I didn't feel like it would be right for me to bring it up. She had done it all for me, and as much as I wanted her to do it again, I wanted it to be her decision.

A big part of me wondered if she was going to surprise me again. During our role-playing, she seemed to get off on calling me when I wasn't expecting it. That was my favorite part too, so if that's what she was planning, I didn't want to ruin the surprise.

There was also the possibility that she knew she had fulfilled my fantasy and was satisfied with that. That would be okay too, but nowhere near as much as the first option.

———

KAYLA

When it came to contact after a man slept with a married woman, I had no idea what the protocol was. I had no clue if I was supposed to send him a thank you message or if he was supposed to send me a fruit basket or something. It was really kind of awkward, so I just waited to see what would happen. It took a few weeks, but I eventually received an email from Kevin.

Kayla,

I hope you aren't offended that I took so long to write you after our night together. This was my first time doing this type of thing and I wasn't sure how to handle things afterwards. I know you're happily married and didn't want to step on any toes or send any wrong impressions by messaging you too eagerly.

With that said, I want you to know that I had a great time with you. You are incredibly sexy and were a lot of fun. I wanted to thank you for such a great time!

Kevin

I thought it was sweet of him to send me a message that basically thanked me for allowing him to fuck me. I smiled reading it and wrote him back quickly.

Kevin,

Thank you so much for your email this morning. I have to admit that I too wasn't sure of what to do after our little get together. I wouldn't have been mad at you if you hadn't written again, but I appreciate the fact that you took the time to do so. I must have made an impression. ;-)

I also had a great time with you that night. As you know, it was my first time doing anything like that and you did a great job making me feel comfortable, safe and secure. You also did a great job with your tongue, but I'm sure you already knew that.

Kayla

I had a smile on my face just knowing that Kevin was a decent guy and was glad I'd come across him to fulfill my husband's fantasy. I thought that was going to be the last I ever heard from him and was surprised when I got another email the next day.

Hey Kayla,

It was great to hear back from you yesterday. I meant to write back last evening, but I was exhausted after a long day.

I'm glad you had as much fun with me as I did with you. I've been thinking a lot about that night since it happened and was wondering if you might like to get together again.

If you're interested, just let me know and we can set something up. Hopefully I'll talk to you soon.

Kevin

I was surprised that he was wanting to see me again, but was extremely flattered. I really did have a great time with him and wouldn't mind doing it again. Of course, that was for selfish reasons. As much fun as I had with him, the real fun for me was all of the fun afterwards with my husband. If it could lead to that kind of sex again, I was definitely up to it.

Kevin,

My husband and I haven't really talked about doing this again, but I wouldn't mind seeing you again either. Let me discuss things with my husband and make sure he's okay with it and then I'll let you know. I'll be in touch soon.

Kayla

26

DILLON

I was sitting on the couch watching a sports documentary when Kayla came home from work. Things were so much different than they were just a few months ago. When she came home, she was actually happy to see me. We were no longer living as strangers in our own home.

"Honey, I got an email today that I wanted to talk to you about," she told me, trying hard to hide the excitement in her voice.

"Are you getting a big promotion where they'll move us to Sicily, giving us a great house and a monthly allowance for your husband?"

"No, but that sure would be nice. Anyway, I got an email from Kevin today."

"Kevin?" I asked, pretending not to know who she was talking about.

"Oh my God, you know who Kevin is. He's the man who was with me while you were in Chicago. He was the one, um, he was the one with me on the FaceTime video."

I thought it was cute that she still couldn't say that Kevin was the man fucking her for me on video.

"Ah yes, I do recall that," I joked. "What did he want?"

"He wanted to know if I wanted to get together again."

"Oh," I said, suddenly getting a little more serious. "What did you say?"

"Well, I basically said that while I had a really great time with him, I'd have to talk to you before I could even entertain the thoughts of seeing him again."

"I appreciate that. So, it sounds like you want to see him again?"

"I'm not really sure. The whole experience was fun and exciting for me and it would be fun to do again. At the same time, I want to make sure that you're okay with it first."

"We haven't really talked about this since that night, have we?"

"No, we've been too busy playing ourselves," she said, poking my nose with her finger.

"All right, well first of all, that night was really hot. I mean, extremely hot. You turned me on more than I'd ever been turned on before. I also appreciated the fact that you were willing to fulfill my fantasy for me. I love you more than you can ever know."

"Aww, I love you too babe," she whispered as she leaned over to give me a kiss.

"With that said, I love how much better our marriage and our sex life have become and I'm happier than I've been in a long time. I'm happy that you fulfilled that fantasy before and I love all the role play we've been doing, but as far as actually doing it again, I really think I've gotten it out of my system."

"All right, that's fine. No big deal," she told me, trying really hard to hide how disappointed she was.

"Are you sure? You don't seem okay?"

"Really, it's fine babe. I love you and if you're over the fantasy, then I'm right there with you. Like you said, this was all about fun, right? Well, it needs to be fun for both of us or it won't be fun for either. You're my priority."

"Thanks for understanding. How did I get so lucky?"

"Sometimes I wonder. I'm gonna jump in the shower before bed. You gonna be up?"

"I'll be waiting in bed for you."

Kayla got up and made her way to the bathroom. I heard her mess around with all kinds of things before the water finally turned on. I waited until I knew for sure that she had gotten in the shower before I grabbed my laptop and opened my email program.

Kevin,

I just talked to her and told her that I had my fantasy fulfilled and was over it. She seemed disappointed, but told me that she was okay with the decision. She doesn't suspect a thing. I'll send you an email tomorrow morning with the rest of the details.

Dillon

27

KAYLA

It was Dillon's turn to pick what we were going to do for our date night, but he was very tight-lipped about what was on the agenda. He only told me to pack a bag because we wouldn't be back home until morning. He also heavily insinuated that I should pack something sexy to wear for him.

Little did he know, I had ordered some new lingerie for him and it just happened to have arrived that morning. It was a lacy black chemise with the hottest pair of crotchless panties that I'd ever seen in my life. I planned on surprising him with them at home, but it might be even more fun to spring them on him during whatever he had planned for us.

We left the house around 3:00 in the afternoon, which was much earlier than we ever left for our dates before. He refused to tell me where we were going, even after I figured out that we were headed downtown. It wasn't until we pulled up in front of The Ambassador Hotel that I finally knew.

"This is something I've wanted to do with you for a long time. We're going to get a room, and we're not coming out until tomorrow morning."

"What about dinner? We have to come out for that, right?"

"We're going to order room service, but we'll worry about that later. Come on inside, or we're going to be late."

Late? We were checking into a hotel. What could we possibly be late for? These were the thoughts in my head as someone rushed out to the car to help with our bags.

I couldn't believe my eyes when we walked in. It was a genuine definition of luxury. There was marble everywhere, and everything was shining as though everything inside was personally polished by hand.

"Hi, we have a reservation for Doctor Dillon Baker," my husband told the woman at the front desk, an attractive blonde without a single hair out of place.

"Yes, Doctor Baker, we've been expecting you. We've got you in room 700, and the gentlemen here will be happy to help you to your room," the woman said, handing a key card to my husband. "Go ahead and get into your home and we'll be ready for you in about twenty minutes."

"What's in twenty minutes?" I whispered to Dillon as we stepped onto the elevator.

"You'll see," he replied with a smirk.

The room itself was fantastic. It was two levels, the top being a large bedroom and the bottom being an over-sized living area and a bathroom with one of the biggest tubs I'd ever seen.

"Oh, I'm getting in that later," I told him.

"Look at the size of that thing. I'm coming with you."

Dillon whisked me out of the room as I was still admiring it and took me back down to the reception area. Two women were standing there holding white robes that were as soft as a cloud.

"Please go into the bathrooms behind you, strip out of your clothes and put on your robes. We'll meet you right around the corner here when you're done," the woman said as she handed us our robes.

The surprise ended up being a 90-minute spa treatment. It was unbelievable. I got a facial, manicure, pedicure, and the most amazing massage I could have imagined. I didn't want it to end, but sadly it had to. Still, I was feeling so relaxed.

"Thank you so much for that, Dillon. I enjoyed that."

"Don't thank me yet; we're just getting started."

We went up to our room and found a bottle of wine chilling in our room. Dillon poured each of us a glass and made the call to order room service. He ordered a Kansas City strip steak with a loaded baked potato for himself while I got grilled chicken with sweet potato fries.

The food was so good, much better than any restaurant we had been to lately. The only thing missing was dessert, and Dillon agreed. He called down to the front desk and requested some chocolate covered strawberries.

"Did you bring something sexy to wear for me?" Dillon asked.

"Why don't you let me slip into the bathroom and change, then you can tell me."

I was still in the bathroom getting ready for him when I heard the knock on the door. Our strawberries had arrived, and I was excited to have them as it's a treat I don't get very often. I slid the panties on, adjusted the chemise, and then burst through the door to make my grand entrance.

That was when I realized that the gentleman from room service was still standing there. I was mortified and was about to rush back into the bathroom before I saw his face. This was no man from room service. It was Kevin.

"Kevin? What in the hell are you doing here?" I asked, stunned to find him standing in the middle of our date.

"Hello, Kayla. Your husband reached out to me and

thanked me for treating you with respect while I was with you. We kind of started talking a bit after that, and he asked if I'd be up for a threesome with the both of you."

"A threesome? Dillon? What's going on? I thought you were over all this stuff?"

"Yeah, about that, I wanted this to be a surprise. We've been emailing back and forth for a bit, and since you seemed to be comfortable with him, I thought he'd be a good choice for something like this. If you're okay with it, I'd like this night to be all about you."

I thought about it for a few moments before deciding what the hell? It was an experience I'd never had, and I liked the idea of being the center of attention.

"All right, if you boys think you can handle me, let's go!"

It didn't take long before all three of us were on the bed. I was positioned between them and was taking turns between kissing Dillon and kissing Kevin. Each man was pawing at me, which made me feel very sexy.

Kevin started grabbing my breasts and kissing all over my neck while Dillon slid his hand between my legs, feeling my freshly shaved pussy already becoming slick with my juices. I knew I was about to have a lot of fun.

"Why don't the two of you get out of those clothes and lay down?" I asked, although it was more of a command.

They each stripped and laid down on the bed on

either side of me. Both were already becoming aroused, and I planned to use that to my advantage.

I grabbed each of their cocks and started stroking them slowly, feeling them getting stiffer in my hand by the second. For the next 15 minutes, I took turns taking one into my mouth while I sucked the other. It was incredible, and I was very, very turned on.

"Why don't you go ahead and lay down now?" Dillon said as he guided me down onto the bed.

Almost immediately, he thrust his cock into my mouth while Kevin positioned himself between my legs so he could eat my pussy. His tongue felt so good running up and down my lips, connecting with my clit at the very top.

He ate me out for a while before Dillon said he wanted in on the action, with Kevin taking his place in my mouth. My husband used the exact same moves he'd used on the night I fucked Kevin and had me coming in what seemed like seconds.

"Fuck, you're too good at that," I yelled as he came up to kiss me.

"You love it, and you know it," he replied.

For the next several hours, both men took turns on me. It seemed to be a competition as every time Kevin would fuck me, Dillon would come right in and try to outdo him. I sure as fuck wasn't going to complain about it. Then an idea popped into my head. It was a fantasy that I hadn't even shared with Dillon.

"I want you both at the same time," I announced.

"Isn't that what we've been doing?" Dillon asked, genuinely confused by my question.

"No, I want you both inside of me at once. One in front, one in back. I want you to share me!"

That made it click for both men. Kevin was already lying on the bed, so I mounted him and slid down his thick, hard cock. Dillon followed suit and maneuvered himself on the bed behind me. After lubing himself up, he pushed his dick into my ass, nearly causing me to shake and topple over.

"Oh my god, you both feel so good," I screamed as I could feel them both moving inside of me.

I felt so completely full, and it was the most intense feeling I'd ever had. Feeling each man moving within, Kevin sliding into me while Dillon slid out and vice versa was crazy. I started to orgasm almost instantly.

"Fuck me harder!" I yelled once I got used to the feeling. "I want you to treat me like your fucking slut."

And that's exactly what they did. They pounded me into oblivion. The fucked me like a slut with a capital s. I lost my bearings and didn't even know where the sounds I was making came from.

The most amazing thing happened right at the end. I

was having my most intense orgasm of the night when both men couldn't take it any longer, and both exploded inside of me. They came so much that I couldn't hold it all in. Their cum was escaping like a faucet all around their cocks.

Once I had drained both of their balls completely empty, Dillon pulled himself out of me, allowing me to dismount Kevin before I collapsed on the bed. I was shaking so hard that I knew there was no way I could have stood up. It didn't matter. Dillon laid down next to me, and I nuzzled into his chest. Kevin didn't stick around. I think he knew that part wasn't for him, but he did thank us for a fun evening.

The entire night was fun, but to me, the best part was right at the end. I was in the arms of the man I loved. The man who had planned such an amazing night for me. A man who was secure enough in himself and our relationship to share me with another man. A man who I knew loved me unconditionally and had gone to great lengths to fix a marriage that was broken and turn it into what it was. I loved him, and I looked forward to spending the rest of my life by his side.

DEREK'S DARK DESIRES

Subscribe to my Dark Desires newsletter and get a FREE copy of Riot instantly! Riot is a full-length novel that is only available to subscribers!

Once you have your free book, you will have the advantage of knowing when I will be releasing my next title, when I'm having special deals, and you'll be the first to know the next time I have some cool stuff to give away (you can unsubscribe at any time).

newsletter.derekmasters.com

ABOUT THE AUTHOR

Derek Masters is an erotic romance author from the Kansas City, MO area. He graduated from the University of Kansas with a degree in criminal justice, but discovered that writing was his true passion. You can often find him talking sports at local hole in the wall bars or working on his next novel in a crowded coffee shop.

www.derekmasters.com
derek@derekmasters.com

ALSO BY DEREK MASTERS

Please check out my website for a complete list of all of my novels. If you enjoyed the book you just read, please consider taking a moment to let me know by leaving a review on Amazon and/or Goodreads. I appreciate your support more than I could ever express!

Facebook: www.facebook.com/authorderekmasters

Fan page: www.facebook.com/derekmasterswrites

Private group: www.facebook.com/groups/dereksdirtysubs

Amazon author page: www.amazon.com/author/derekmasters

Website: derekmasters.com

Email: derek@derekmasters.com

Made in the USA
Middletown, DE
23 June 2021